Timothy Brum

Printed and bound by Lightning Source, Milton Keynes, UK

Published by Crossbridge Books
Berrow Green, Martley
WR6 6PL
Tel: +44 (0)1886 821128
www.crossbridgebooks.com

ISBN 978-0-9561787-3-2

British Library Cataloguing in Publication Data.
A catalogue record for this book is available from the
British Library.

TIMOTHY BRUM

R M MACE

CROSSBRIDGE BOOKS

For Alice

Part One

Birmingham

Timothy was three. He knew he was three because his mummy would say things like, "Now you are three, Timothy, you should be able to remember to say 'thank you'." Timothy knew his name. It was Timothy Nathaniel Whittaker. But if someone asked him his name he never quite got past Nathaniel. Adding Whittaker was just too long. Timothy knew his bear was called Bear. He was gripping his paw tightly. Timothy knew something else as well. His knee was hurting where he had fallen over and banged it... and he wanted his mummy. The kind lady holding his hand was asking him his name.

"Timothy... Nath... an... i... el."

The kind lady was taking him somewhere. He hoped his mummy would come soon.

*

Cardiff

Gwen typed the 'Lost Child' information into the computer. Name. Gwen typed Timothy Nathaniel... The handwritten piece of paper she had been given said: 'found in Brum'. Gwen looked at the word 'Brum' and said to herself, "Oh yes, it's short for Birmingham." She typed Brum.

1

Gwen saved the document as she went along and was glad she had when the network crashed for the third time that day. By the time the system was back online and Gwen had finished her coffee break and her chat with Helen, she had forgotten to forward the document.

*

Birmingham

Timothy knew his name was Timothy Nathaniel Whittaker, but Timothy Brum was much easier to say. So when a friendly young man asked him if his name was Timothy Brum, he said yes. After all, he was tired and he badly wanted his mummy. Timothy knew he was hungry because he had a pain in his tummy. He knew something else too... he was frightened.

*

Birmingham six years later

Tim walked out the door with his usual rucksack on his back. He walked away from the house in the direction of the train station. The sun was shining and there was a gentle breeze. It was a lovely day for an adventure. Everything in the street was carrying on as normal. No one noticed him. No one was interested. No one saw the excitement on his face. He walked to the station. Today it didn't seem very far away.

Tim strolled nonchalantly onto the platform. It didn't matter that he had no money for a ticket. If anyone stopped him he would give his address and the fine would be sent there. That was their problem. He didn't care.

The first train that arrived was going to Redditch. Tim knew that he could get off at Barnt Green (where there was no ticket office) and walk to a service station by the motorway. Tim found a seat, sat down and pulled out a packet of biscuits. As he did so a scruffy-looking Bear fell out onto his lap. Tim giggled to himself, glanced around quickly to make sure no one had noticed that he had brought his Bear and stuffed him back in the rucksack. Bear was his very own. He had always had him. No one had managed to take him away from Tim, although he had been the cause of many a fight at the home.

Tim watched the city disappear as fields with sheep and late crops came into view. The train squealed to a halt. Tim stepped off the train at the same time as a young mum struggling with two children and a buggy. He walked through the car park and down to where the shops were. He didn't have a clue which way to walk. He would have to ask. He went into a bakery, drawn by the delicious smell of freshly cooked bread and cakes.

"Excuse me, which way do I go from here to get to the motorway?"

The girl behind the counter looked at him in surprise.

"Are you walking there?" she questioned. "It's a long way."

"It's for a school project," Tim lied.

The girl gave him directions and said she hoped he could remember it all. As he left, he heard her muttering that the stupid school should have provided a map. Tim found the directions easy to follow, especially when he reached the first roundabout where the motorway was signposted. It took longer than he expected and the last part seemed to be all uphill. By the time he got to the exit road of the service station Tim was tired, hungry and not nearly as excited.

But he had come prepared. He had pinched several packets of biscuits and a couple of bags of crisps from the kitchen before he left. He had also made a sign to hold up with the word 'LONDON' clearly printed on it. So Tim sat and waited... and waited.

Most of the people in the cars that went by looked the other way and pretended that they hadn't seen him. A few families went by. One little boy smiled and waved at him. Another boy pulled a face and stuck out his tongue. But mostly he was ignored.

After about two hours (which is a long time for a nine year

old) a truck pulled up. Tim got to his feet and walked over. He looked up into the face of a man who was smiling at him. Tim climbed up onto a step and peered into the cabin. He could now see that there were two men in there. The driver slowly looked Tim over in a way that made him feel very uncomfortable. He had seen that look before and knew all too well what it meant. He then noticed the pictures plastered around the dashboard of men and boys in strange poses. Tim felt that familiar feeling of nausea rising as he tried to block out the memories. He jumped down and ran, the sound of laughter roaring in his ears. For the first time that day Tim felt some doubt about his adventure.

Another two hours went by. His biscuits and crisps long since gone, he was feeling very hungry and beginning to feel cold and stiff from sitting in one place for so long. A small blue car went by. The driver looked at him and then away. He watched the car slow a bit, and then accelerate again, then slow again, as if someone were trying to make up their mind about whether to stop or not. Then the car did stop. Tim wasn't sure if it was for him, so he just sat still. Then the passenger door was pushed open from inside. Tim got up and walked cautiously to the car. Standing a safe distance away this time he peered in. He could see a small elderly lady smiling at him.

"Are you going to London?" he called.

"I'm going round the M25 to Croydon to visit an old friend, so I could drop you somewhere," she called back.

Tim decided to take the risk and get into the car. It was warm, comfortable and smelled of flowers. This was OK.

*

Worcestershire

Christine Whittaker was a busy mum. In the morning she walked her son Jake to the local primary school. On the way she collected two boys from next door because their mum had to get off early to work. It was only a few hundred yards away, but even in this quiet village in rural Worcestershire no one let their children walk to school unaccompanied. A lot of the mums had to drive in from further away and had to park in the church or pub car parks and then walk the short distance to the school. There was usually a chance to chat with some of the other mums; Jenny was nearly always there with her twins.

Christine allowed her fifteen-year-old daughter to walk up to the High School (just opposite the primary school) with her friends. Emma was in her last year at the High School and would soon be sixteen. At one time Christine and her husband Paul had expected to be able to pay for Emma's A-level education. There were some very good schools in Worcester and Paul had a good job with an accounting firm in Birmingham. But the credit crunch had hit them just as it had hit everybody else. Emma had been looking forward to earning some extra spending money when she got to sixteen by waitressing at the local pub, but times had changed and the landlord was cutting down the hours of his existing staff. There wasn't much for teenagers to do in the village and without the extra money she would find it difficult to pay for excursions into Worcester.

When Christine and Paul had moved to Martley, they had taken on a huge mortgage. They were both working and their future seemed secure. But Christine had not been able to continue working after they had lost Timothy and was only now, after all these years, pulling herself out of a deep depression. Paul had been very supportive, suppressing his own sadness, but there were now times when the stress began to show. All the previous luxuries were gradually being shed. Christine was still driving the kids to and from their out of school sports activities, but she knew this would have to stop soon, and she worried about the consequences.

Once she was home, Christine would begin cleaning, washing and cooking in advance so that she could help the kids with their homework later. On fine days she kept the garden under control and there always seemed to be paperwork to attend to. The post only ever seemed to bring bills and statements that needed checking and then everything had to be shredded. Several days a week she would have to shop and queue for petrol in the city. It always amazed her how much time it all took.

By three o'clock Christine was back at the school gates to collect Jake and 'the boys', as she tended to call them. She looked after them most days until their mum came home from work. There was a very good after-school club but it meant that Jake had someone to play with after school, so the arrangement worked out well for everyone.

Today was much the same as any other day. Christine walked back into the kitchen after dropping the boys at school. The sun was shining but there was a cold nip in the autumn air. She went and stood by the Aga to warm herself. For the umpteenth time she wondered if Timothy was warm. A body had never been found and Christine was convinced in her heart that he was still alive out there somewhere. For years she had gone back to where she had last seen him on that fateful shopping day in Birmingham. She had spent hours tracing and retracing their steps. She had carried a photograph of him and asked Joe Public and all the shop assistants if they had seen him. She had demanded to search through hours of CCTV footage. She had trawled through cyberspace in search of him. She had pestered all the police stations. Timothy had become a cold case.

Cold… Christine couldn't cope with the thought that he might be out there somewhere lonely and cold. She clung to the hope that a kind family had adopted him. She would fantasise about him being with a rich family and going to the best schools and becoming someone famous when he was older. Christine gave herself a shake. "Come on Chris," she said to herself, "make yourself useful to the children who *are* here." In this way, as on most days, she forced herself into activity lest she begin brooding again.

*

At first the old lady said nothing to him. They had been driving for about ten minutes before she began with the inevitable questions. Tim had a ready answer for everything.

In the years since his family had been lost to him Tim had plenty of time to invent a family of his own. He imagined a mother who was tall, slim and brunette; who had been an actress but had given it all up to devote herself to her family. His father was tall, handsome and well-built. He was in business and drove around in a Porsche. Tim had invented an older brother, Carl, who was in London training to become a pro-footballer. They owned a house in London, a house in Birmingham and a villa in Spain where they could go for their holidays anytime they liked.

Conveniently, Tim's imaginary mother had been a stage actress, so only people who went regularly to the theatre would have heard of her; she wasn't that famous. His brother was in the under-eighteen squad, so people wouldn't have heard of him yet. Tim's imaginary family was so familiar to him that the lies he told about them hardly seemed untrue. His words came so easily and without hesitation that anyone listening had no reason to doubt the story.

"So why are you hitchhiking on your own like this? It's terribly dangerous; surely your family must be worried," wondered the dear old lady.

Tim continued his story, finding it very easy. Lying was one of the skills he had learned in the children's home very early on. He feigned surprise. "I'm going to visit my brother. Mum and Dad were so busy I didn't want to bother them. Do you think they'll be worried? Maybe we can stop at the next service station, and if you would be kind enough to lend me some money, I could ring Mum and tell her I'm safe and she can ring my brother and get him to meet me at the station. Do you think that's the best thing to do?"

Tim turned his innocent gaze towards the lady and looked up at her with appealing eyes. She immediately relaxed and said that it was an excellent idea, that she had enough change and she would treat him to a meal at the same time. Now that she was no longer worrying about this small waif that she had picked up, she began to chatter to him, mostly about her own childhood.

She talked about how she used to play in the farmer's field, and climb the apple trees, scrumping at this time of year. She told about playing with friends and going for cycle rides. She described in minute detail the birthday when her father had made her the most exquisite doll's house with opening doors and windows and it even had a staircase. She stopped talking as they pulled into the service station.

Inside she gave Tim a handful of change and hurried off to the ladies. Tim pocketed the money for later use and went into the gents.

A couple of hours later Tim strolled into East Croydon station. It wasn't difficult for a nine-year-old boy to attach himself to a large family and drift past the ticket office. He got onto a train to Victoria and settled himself into a corner. He was well fed, warm and comfortable. Right now he felt pleased with himself.

*

London

Old Simon's story was an old-fashioned one. He had been a successful salesman with a wife and two children. When his older child was ten, his wife left with another man and took the children with her. Simon began to drink alone in the evenings. He had to pay a lot of maintenance money to his ex-wife to support the children, but he still had a house and a job.

Then one day as he was driving home, not fully concentrating, his life took an unexpected knock. He was turning left at a difficult junction. He had checked the traffic in all directions and was accelerating around the bend. He hadn't noticed the small boy stepping onto the zebra crossing just a few metres away. He hit the boy. The boy's leg was broken and the mother sued. The police had carried out a routine breath test and found that the alcohol limit was just below the legal limit. But the magistrate ruled that he had been driving without due care and attention and told him that he was lucky to get away with just a ban. He was given a three-year ban and consequently lost his job. He couldn't pay his mortgage. He lost his house. He couldn't get a new job because no one would give him a reference.

So began a downward spiral. He drank more, ate less and quickly found himself homeless and friendless. That was twenty years ago. Now he was a veteran of the streets of London. He knew all the safe places to sleep. He knew where to get a free meal and the best place to get enough money to buy a drink. He never stole and tried to stay within the law, sleeping in places where he wouldn't be told to move on. He got himself a free shower in the sports clubs and kept himself clean.

Now Old Simon saw young ones joining him on the streets. They weren't like the old ones who had a story to tell. These youngsters had no story… no childhood, no family, no education, no work, no prospects, no future. Their lives were ruled by drugs and they survived by crime. They wouldn't think twice about stealing from the old ones, and if you got in their way the knives would come out. Simon knew quite a few of the old ones who had died that way.

Simon was in the gents at Victoria Station. He was having a wash and brushing his teeth with an old brush, which was so splayed that it would make his gums bleed. He prided himself on his ability to keep clean no matter how far he had fallen. Today, just like every other day, he would begin his rounds, meeting up with old friends and calling in for his 'freebies' on the way. He began stowing things away inside his voluminous coat and noticed a small boy who had just emerged from a cubicle. He looked as if he had slept there all night.

Tim had spent a rough night. The platform at Victoria had been crowded. He was short for his age and didn't have a clue which direction to follow. He found himself dragged along by the surging crowd, past the ticket gate and into an open area where the crowds began to disperse. He had managed to squeeze through the barrier next to a lady with a buggy. He used the change the old lady had given him to get a chocolate bar from a vending machine. He sat down on a bench to consider his next move. A fat man sat next to him. He had beads of sweat on his forehead and smelled of cigarette smoke.

"Working?" he asked.

"My mum is just in the ladies," Tim lied.

It worked; the fat man flushed and hurried away, clutching his briefcase to himself as if someone had tried to steal it. Tim had to find somewhere safe for the night. Somewhere he wouldn't be pestered by any more sweaty men.

Tim squeezed under the turnstile and went into the gents. He found the furthest cubicle and locked himself in. Every now and again he flushed the toilet in case a supervisor came in. He curled up in the corner, wedged between the toilet pan and the wall. It stank, but it was safe.

Tim managed to ignore most of the steady stream of visitors. Then the cubicle next to his became occupied. Someone was smoking something heavy. He had smelled this before at the children's home. Some of the older boys were smoking rocks. He heard someone else come in. He must have been a dealer; he was selling to the first person.

Suddenly there was a commotion, doors banging and angry voices. Tim couldn't understand what was being said but there was a lot of swearing and shouting. A body was slammed up against the door of his cubicle. Below the door he could see the feet of the victim twisting and turning in his struggle. Tim had stopped breathing. He could feel the blood pounding in his ears as the adrenaline screamed through his veins. He had only one thought: "Don't let the door open." He picked out some words: stingers... phoney crack... Yardies... Colombian necktie. With each expletive came the sound of a punch, followed by a whimper. Eventually it stopped. The beaten man slumped to the floor. Tim watched the hands and knees of the man as he crawled away, smearing blood on the floor as he went. Tim told himself to breathe. No one knew he was there. He had survived.

The silence was broken every now and again by sweaty men bringing in young girls for their pleasure. Tim heard the grunting and forced back the nausea. In the early hours, out of sheer exhaustion, he finally drifted into a fitful sleep.

When he awoke he was cold, stiff and hungry. He was intensely aware of the stench of dried urine. He was terrified of what might be behind the door. He forced himself to open it and then froze. In front of him was a huge hairy man looking directly at him. Tim's throat seemed to squeeze into a knot. He couldn't even move his legs.

"Want some breakfast?" came the gruff voice of this hairy mountain of a man.

Tim's brain struggled to understand. Was he being friendly? The hairy face smiled. Tim began to relax. His legs could move now and he stepped over the patch of dried blood. He stood, looked up into the hairy face, and felt hope.

*

Worcestershire

Celia's little blue car pulled up on the drive. She pulled on the handbrake and sighed. It was a long drive and she was glad to be home. It had been very nice visiting Joan, but now she looked forward to a nice cup of tea, in her favourite cup, in her own comfy chair.

Celia's husband had died of a heart attack a few years ago. Of course she had been devastated at first. But she had surprised both herself and her friends by her quick recovery. She had joined the Women's Institute and a couple of other ladies' clubs. She was rather ashamed to admit it to herself, but she enjoyed being able to watch TV without having to wait until the cricket or rugby had finished.

Pulling her bags off the passenger seat, Celia's thoughts went back to her little waif. As she carried the bags through her front door she pictured his mother being reunited with her son. She imagined him telling her about Celia giving him a lift and thought how thankful she must have felt towards her.

Celia put on the kettle and looked at the clock. Good, she would be able to watch one of her favourite programmes. Sitting in her comfy armchair, cup of tea and biscuits to hand, Celia switched on the TV. The music played out for the programme 'Where are you?' The smiling faces of the presenters June and George appeared on the screen. Celia took a mouthful of biscuit and a sip of tea.

"On tonight's programme," announced June, "we have a very sad story that goes back to six years ago in Birmingham. Our special guest is Christine Whittaker and she will tell her story in her own words." Celia sat sipping her tea and listened while Christine told the nation how she had lost Timothy. She described him as he had been when he was just three. She described Bear in great detail and then broke down and wept in front of millions of onlookers.

Celia wondered how a mother coped with such an awful loss. She was so glad her little waif wouldn't be one of those 'lost' children that fed this programme with their stories. The credits rolled up the screen and Celia went into the kitchen to get another cup of tea. She then settled back into her armchair to enjoy the next episode of *EastEnders*, and put the little waif out of her mind.

*

The whole Whittaker family had sat and watched as 'Where are you?' went out on air. Christine wept again and Emma joined her. Jake had never known his brother; he had only been a tiny baby. But Emma had helped her mum with Timothy. Emma was six when Timothy was born and had enjoyed playing 'mum'. She had pushed him in his buggy, helped with his nappies and played endlessly with him. She felt his loss almost as much as her mother did.

The credits rolled up the screen and they all sat in anticipation. Surely someone somewhere must know something. They sat for an hour, almost without talking, hoping the phone would ring. Nothing. Another hour went by. No one dared use the phone. Still nothing.

Emma had tried not to blame her mum. She understood how easy it must have been. Her mum was distracted by the baby and had taken her eyes off Timothy for just a moment. Christine had tried taking Emma to bereavement counselling, but it wasn't much help. Emma had blamed herself for not wanting to go shopping with her mum that day. Instead she had gone to a friend's house to play. This guilt had turned to anger over the years, which was usually directed towards her mum. Christine put her daughter's behaviour down to being a teenager, but it had a deeper root.

Emma decided that the atmosphere at home was too intense. She wanted to go out. There wasn't anywhere in the village for her age group unless you wanted to hang out by the off licence. She and her friends would get together with some of the older ones who were already driving. They would all pile into a car and head into Worcester to go clubbing. Using fake or borrowed IDs and wearing the right clothes, they could usually get in.

Emma sent a text to Sarah and within half an hour she was queuing outside the bigger of Worcester's two nightclubs. Although Emma didn't have a job yet, her dad was able to give her a decent amount of pocket money. She was able to pay to get in and buy drinks. Emma had asked her mum to send her a text if anything happened. She would try to put Timothy out of her mind while she was out and just have fun.

All Emma's friends went clubbing regularly. Many of them would buy a bottle of cheap wine to drink before they went out, to get them started. These girls wore miniskirts and low-cut tops. Their aim was to pull as many guys as they could and try to get an older boyfriend who had a car and money. A friend of one of Emma's friends came up to them.

"I saw your mum on the telly. Have you had any luck?" she asked in a friendly way.

"Not yet. Thanks for asking," replied Emma.

The next question didn't feel so friendly.

"Smoke?"

Emma knew all about this girl. She lived in Malvern and came from a rich family. Copying some of the other teenagers around her, the combination of money and boredom had led to her trying crack; she got hooked. It was easy to guess where she got the money to feed her habit: "Daddy, the price of drinks has gone up in the club; can I please have some more money?"

Others became dealers, selling to the kids in the more deprived areas to pay for their habit. And it wasn't just crack; Emma had heard about kids on heroin. One thing Emma was never going to do was drugs. She had already seen it destroy the lives of kids at her school. One of her close friends had become schizophrenic. But she had to be careful about how she replied.

"Thanks but I don't need any right now. I need to keep my head clear in case I get a phone call." The girl accepted this and left them.

When Emma let herself in at three in the morning there were no messages. Her parents had evidently stayed up later than usual. There were signs of a late night supper. Emma tiptoed upstairs and peered into Timothy's room. It hadn't changed in all these years. She took off her makeup, crawled into bed and cried herself to sleep.

14

London

Old Simon didn't ask any questions. That way this young one wouldn't have to tell him any lies. He knew that this boy was too young to be allowed to sleep rough. The hostels wouldn't take him. He had heard about a refuge in London somewhere that helped young runaways. But they would most likely send him back to wherever he had run away from. He might be sent to a foster family or into care. Simon had heard enough horror stories about these places to make him think the boy would be safest with him for now.

Simon had seen many young ones appear on the streets. Within a few hours they would be approached by drug pushers or pimps. They would be offered an easy life or a way out of their misery. It always led to addiction and crime. Perhaps Simon was reminded of his own son when he looked at this forlorn child. For some reason he wanted to help this one. This time he wanted a different story. Perhaps he was just being selfish. A small boy tagging along could be useful. He might get more sympathy from those who gave handouts, especially if they were women. Either way, reasoned Simon, it would be better for the boy to stick with him for now.

Simon followed a well-trodden route, threading his way through the crowds. Every now and then he would check over his shoulder that the boy was still following. Over the years Simon had been befriended by an elderly lady who worked in a bakery. She was a churchgoer and hoped that her kindness to him might someday win him over for the church. Simon was happy to have long debates with her. He had plenty of time on his hands and she was always good for breakfast.

This morning he arrived at the back door with the small boy in tow. They were invited right into the warm steamy kitchen. Simon congratulated himself on his forward thinking. His friend at the bakery fussed and clucked over them. This morning they were offered hot drinks as well as food. His friend didn't ask any questions, she just gave them what they needed. This morning Simon wondered if perhaps there really was something in this church business.

Their next stop was the nearest Salvation Army hostel. It was a long walk for the boy. Simon had to keep slowing down so that the boy could keep up. They didn't speak at all. His question, "Want a sleeping bag?" was rhetorical. Outside, Simon told the boy to wait nearby.

"If they see you they'll try to send you back where you came from. They'll think it's the right thing to do, but I guess you must have had a good reason to run away."

The boy looked glad to sit and rest on the nearby steps. Simon didn't take long; he knew all the workers here. This morning he was suddenly acutely aware of how kind these people were. They just gave the sleeping bags out for free. They even smiled and talked to you like a human being. Maybe it was because for the first time in twenty years Simon was caring about someone else. For the second time this morning, Simon wondered again about this church business.

With the sleeping bag safely tucked away inside his over-large coat, Simon set off towards Hyde Park, indicating to the boy to follow. Simon found a bench so they could rest. He still didn't ask any questions. If the boy wanted to talk, he would when he was ready. That would be when he trusted him. Runaways found it difficult to trust. It wasn't hard to see why.

*

Tim was very hungry when the hairy man asked if he wanted breakfast. He decided to follow at a safe distance. He kept close as they threaded through the crowds outside the station. He kept a little further away once there were fewer people.

Tim decided that he must be some sort of tramp. He had kind eyes in that hairy face. When the man ducked into a dark alley Tim hesitated. The man turned and checked that Tim was

16

still there. Tim decided to risk it and follow him. He reckoned he could outrun this big man if he had to.

At the bakery Tim relaxed. It was warm and smelled delicious. A kind elderly lady gave him a huge breakfast of sausages, fried egg, baked beans and toast. *And* a steaming cup of sweet tea. She kept calling him "Deary" and smiled at him with wet eyes. Tim wondered if his grandmother was like her. Then he thought about his mum. Whenever Tim met a 'motherly' woman he wondered about his mum. His throat would tighten. His eyes would sting. His teeth would clench. He dug his fingers into his hands until the pain took the thoughts away.

This morning Tim's hunger took the thoughts away. He looked down at the plate and tucked in. He didn't look up again until he had scraped up every last morsel. Then he looked up to see the kind lady's old wrinkly face beaming down at him. "You must'a' needed that, Deary. How about another cuppa?"

Tim had eaten a lot at the bakery. He was getting a stitch trying to keep up with the hairy man. He wasn't used to walking so far. He began to worry that he might lose him. This tramp was his only friend in London… or anywhere. Eventually they stopped. Tim sat on some steps and felt his feet throbbing. His old trainers were rubbing on the tops of his toes. He guessed that he probably had blisters. He had hardly recovered before he was chasing after the hairy man again. Fortunately it wasn't long before they stopped again. This time it was a park bench. Tim flopped down and wondered how far he would have to walk today. He took off a trainer and saw a tiny spot of blood on his sock. He had guessed right.

"Eat this!" said the hairy man. It was more of a command than an offer. He was holding out a doughnut. Tim could see

17

the jam dripping out. It must have been squashed in a coat pocket. Tim took it gladly and began to nibble on it to make it last. Tim spoke for the first time.

"What's your name?" he asked.

"Simon," came the reply. "What's yours?"

"Tim... and thanks."

They reverted to silence.

Part Two

London

Over the next few days Tim followed Simon on his regular weekly routine. That first afternoon they strolled past Buckingham Palace. Simon said they had plenty of time so they went to look at the Houses of Parliament. Tim didn't really know what a Prime Minister was. Simon explained that really he was more important than the Queen, because he made decisions about how things had to be done. Tim still didn't know what a Prime Minister was, but he thought the Houses of Parliament were more impressive than Buckingham Palace. Next they followed the river down to the Tate Gallery. Simon said it was one of his favourite freebies. It was warm and dry, somewhere to sit and lots to look at.

In the Tate Britain they had a quick look at some old portraits. Tim said they made him feel miserable, especially the ones of families. Instead they went to look at the Turner exhibition. Simon said he liked the ones of Switzerland because he had always wanted to go there. Tim liked the one of a steamer. But they sat longest in front of 'Moonlight, a study at Millbank'. They both liked this one. "It's hard to believe this place where we are now looked just like that when Mr Turner was painting. That's the Thames just outside here," observed Simon. "In those days there were no cars, no TVs, no computers, no video games, no mobile phones, not even a radio," Simon continued.

"What did people do?" wondered Tim. It sounded very boring.

"They walked or used horses. A bit like us really; we walked everywhere today. We had a chat with friends. We even listened to live music in the park. It's as if we've gone back in time."

They left the gallery and sat on the steps outside, so they could look at the same view that Turner did. "If you could really travel in time, where would you go?" asked Tim. If Simon could have changed history he would have gone back to the day he knocked down that little boy. Instead he said, "I'd like to see what the future will be like in about two hundred years from now. See what gadgets they've invented. See if anyone is living on Mars yet. What would you do?"

"I'd go back to…" Tim's voice trailed away. He tried to think how he would find out which day to go back to. No one had any record of that day. People remembered that he had been found in Birmingham, looking for his mummy. But there seemed to be no information on any of the computer systems. He was a mystery. "I don't know," said Tim, "I can't remember." Simon didn't ask any more questions.

They spent that evening collecting things for Tim's 'sleepover'. A hat, some cardboard, some bread trays and some old newspapers all went into a big canvas bag. They went to a late night soup kitchen for some hot food to keep them warm for the night. Simon took Tim to a basement, which was dry and quiet, and showed Tim how to make a bed from their collection.

So began a week in which Tim learned how to live rough. He was happily unaware that Simon's continued presence kept him safe from the many predators lurking on the streets. Tim learned that he could travel for free on the bendy bus if he got on with a family. Simon explained that this would be safe because they had CCTV. He learned that he would probably get caught if he tried the tube without a ticket. Simon didn't like the tube; there were too many pickpockets, and there was a good chance you'd get arrested for something you didn't do, just because you didn't look right. Taxis were for people with money. So it was walk or hop on a bus if you were lucky.

Tim's biggest problem was that he couldn't go into most of

the places where Simon got his freebies. He would have to wait outside and hope Simon could bring something out to him. Mostly he came out with something: a warm jacket; a spare hat; food and drinks. Tim couldn't risk being seen. He didn't want to go back to the home. Tim had hated it there. People never knew what to do with him. He couldn't be adopted because he had a family somewhere. He couldn't be fostered because he had never officially been taken into care. When someone tried to find somewhere else for him to go, they always gave up because there were no records. Tim hadn't just been lost by his family. He'd been lost by the system. The computer said he didn't exist, therefore he didn't. If he wasn't there, no one could have him.

Most of the other kids came from families that had broken down. Often something awful had happened. They were 'rescued' by social workers. Often these kids said they would rather have stayed at home even if they were being beaten. Some were there because they had committed a crime and were too young to be locked away. The older ones smoked and did drugs. Some got their money by 'working' on the streets; others simply stole.

The other kids had visitors who would bring presents. Tim got nothing. He watched other families shouting and fighting. Tim didn't even have a family to fight with. Everything he had or used belonged to the home. He owned nothing… except Bear. Bear was his only possession. Bear was his only link with the past. Bear was often pinched by someone, but he always managed to get him back, no matter how much it hurt. Once, there had been only one way to get Bear back. Tim was sick afterwards. He got Bear back. The man was sent away. Tim wasn't going back.

Instead, Tim made himself learn the names of all the roads they walked down so he would be able to find them again. He learned the names of Simon's friends. He learned how to make a warm bed and where to get a late night supper. He learned by heart the route that Simon took each day of the week.

Simon showed Tim how to recognise when a drug deal was

going down so that he could keep as far away as possible. He learned to recognise the signs of a mugging. Simon knew all too well how easy it would be for Tim to get caught up with a crime. If Tim got arrested he would be taken back. Simon was a good teacher. He had twenty years' experience. Tim was determined to learn it all.

*

In the basement of a terrace just north west of Hyde Park, a door slammed. A fifteen-year-old girl walked up the steps. Kelly was dressed in her working clothes: shiny black high-heeled shoes; a tight black mini skirt; a low-cut T shirt; all fishnet and leather. Kelly's story was simple. It wouldn't take long to tell, if anyone bothered to listen. She came from an ordinary family, from an ordinary estate. Her father drank too much, but her family were law abiding. When Kelly was still small her father had left. A new man arrived in the house. When she was eleven she began smoking grass because everyone else at school did. Soon they were trying Ex, which they got from the man on the corner of her road. At fourteen she was skiving school with her boyfriend who gave her tots of methadone. It wasn't long before he persuaded her to try heroin. When she found she needed it, he sold it to her in exchange for her body. Her family had tried to help. She had been sent to clinics and hospitals. Before she was fifteen her mum had kicked her out because of the effect on her younger siblings. Kelly needed money to feed her addiction. There was a simple solution.

Tonight Kelly was heading towards Marble Arch. She had few thoughts. She didn't think much these days. She hoped she had used enough makeup to disguise her pale, unhealthy-looking skin. She hoped the hair extensions would stay in. Her hair had become limp and thin. She hoped more than anything that she would have the energy to earn enough money to pay the dealer.

At about two in the morning Kelly was with her fourth client.

He drove her to a deserted basement. Kelly much preferred to work somewhere warm and comfortable, but he was well-dressed and drove an expensive-looking car. There was no one about. He told her to get out of the car and stand by the wall. It was cold. The ground was hard. Then the pain began. It was unbearable. Kelly had no strength to defend herself and, strangely, no desire to. She simply wanted it to end. He finished. Kelly stretched out her hand to grasp the money which had been tossed on to the concrete ground. Then she curled into a ball and didn't move.

*

Something woke Tim. He lay in the semi-darkness and listened. Old Simon was snoring next to him. That hadn't woken him. He could hear a car engine running somewhere nearby. Tim lay still and listened. Should he wake Simon? He would wait and see. He heard car doors opening and shutting. He heard a man's voice. It sounded far enough away and Tim relaxed a bit. Then he heard a cry of pain. Tim went rigid in his sleeping bag. There was another cry of pain and then a whimper. Tim wanted to wake Simon but he daren't move. He didn't want whoever was there to hear him. He tried not to listen. He tried to listen only to Simon snoring. It didn't work.

It stopped. Tim heard the sound of a car door slamming. The car drove away. Tim could still hear the whimpering. He gave Simon a nudge. Simon grunted and mumbled but stayed asleep. Tim gave him a push. Simon made an angry noise and turned over. Tim wriggled out of his sleeping bag. He checked that Bear was safely hidden. Then he began to walk cautiously to where the sound was coming from. He could see something huddled in a dark corner at the far end. Tim went a little closer. He could see someone curled in a ball and rocking. Tim looked around. He couldn't see anyone else. He went closer. He looked down into a face that was bruised and swollen. There seemed to be blood smeared around the mouth. He could tell it was a girl from the hair and clothes. Her shirt looked as if it had been torn. Tim could see dark red lines across her shoulders. He noticed a jacket lying nearby. He tenderly wrapped the jacket around the wounded shoulders. Tim didn't say anything. He didn't ask any questions. Instead he just sat down next to her and waited.

After a while, she spoke.

"I'm cold," she whispered.

"Can you walk?" asked Tim.

"I don't know. My legs feel numb."

"If you can walk a little way over there, you can share my sleeping bag," offered Tim.

Wincing in obvious pain and limping on one leg, she followed Tim to where he and Simon had constructed their beds for the night. Tim began to rearrange the boxes so that two could just squeeze on. He opened the sleeping bag to make a cover for two. "I can't work with this face," she said, "I don't think I can walk home right now. Thanks." Tim didn't understand what she meant. He knew she needed help.

*

Simon's body had a built-in alarm clock. He would wake around 5.30 every morning. This always gave him time to clear himself and his bed away before anyone else arrived on the scene. This morning was no different. Simon didn't like waking Tim so early. He always seemed to be so tired. He never complained, but Simon could tell from his breathing that he was often almost sleepwalking. It wasn't safe to linger. They could be arrested and questioned. Then Tim would be taken away. He began packing away his things, giving Tim a few minutes more. Then he moved across to wake him.

In the half light Simon couldn't understand what he was looking at. Tim appeared to have strands of long blond hair mingled in with his own. He seemed to have acquired a third arm. Simon leapt back in surprise when he realised there was a second person snuggled inside the sleeping bag. Cautiously he went back and gently lifted the edge of the cover with his long bony finger. The face was still bruised and swollen but he could tell that it was a girl. She looked very young.

Simon told himself to walk away and leave them. He told himself that it would be madness to get involved. He reminded himself how hard it was to survive just on his own. He wondered what had possessed him to get involved with this boy in the first place. He should have known it would be trouble, and now this.

He had been walking round in circles. He hadn't walked away. The weird thing was that since the boy had been with him, his days had found purpose. He had a reason to be. He even thought about the future; not very far, mostly to the next place to sleep. He realised he didn't want that to change.

Simon woke them up. This time it was the girl who leapt in fright.

*

Kelly woke up to see a huge hairy man looming over her. She sat bolt upright and uttered a strangled shriek. The huge man stepped backwards, a look of horror in his eyes. The hairy giant seemed more scared of her. She made herself calm down. The boy next to her sat up. "Be quiet you idiot, someone will hear you screeching like that," he said in a very irritated voice. His hair was sticking up and he looked very cross. Kelly pulled a face at him. The boy pulled one back, using his fingers to try to make an even worse one. There followed a gurning competition, which ended when the big man began laughing. He had an infectious laugh, so they all laughed. At least Kelly would have done if her face hadn't hurt so much.

"Breakfast," the man suddenly announced. Instantly the boy began packing away the boxes and sleeping bag. He was well practised. It only took him a minute. Kelly watched in fascination. Then the two began to walk away. After about ten metres, the boy stopped and turned around. "C'mon," he called. Kelly decided to follow them. She was in no rush to go back to the apartment. She would probably get another beating there for being stupid enough to get her face bashed in. It would be an expensive mistake.

Kelly followed them closely. She had no idea which way they were going. It was still very quiet on the streets. There were a few delivery vans. Some people were going off to an early shift, or leaving a late one. They came to the back door of a bakery. An elderly woman was just unlocking the doors.

"Hello Deary," she said and beamed at the boy. "Come and sit down. I'll have something for you in a jiffy."

Kelly went slowly to the door. The others sat at a table and looked across at Kelly expectantly. The woman followed their gaze. She made a clucking sound and took hold of Kelly's arm and drew her in. "Simon, where did you find this poor little chick with the battered face? You come in and sit down," she continued without waiting for an answer. She fussed around and clucked a great deal. Kelly leaned across and whispered to the boy.

"She's so much like a hen I wouldn't be surprised if she laid an egg."

The boy laughed and said she was like a gran to him.

"Your real name isn't Deary is it?" she asked.

"Tim," he replied, and tucked into his breakfast.

"I'm Kelly," she said, "not Little Chick". They both giggled.

*

Worcestershire

Christine was sitting in her quiet kitchen having a mid-morning coffee. Today was housework day. She didn't particularly like it. Neither did she resent it. Cleaning was simply something that had to be done. Over the years she had noticed that the children, especially Jake, were much calmer and less irritable after school when the house was neat and tidy. Emma would walk through the door, take a deep breath and say, "Mmm, I like the smell of polish."

Christine found it quite relaxing herself. Yes, it made her physically tired, but it was not a stressful day. She wasn't checking the time every few minutes. She sipped her coffee. Gradually she became aware that she could hear a dripping sound. She put down her coffee and began walking round the kitchen to find the source of the sound. A leaky radiator. Bother, it had already created quite a puddle. She put a bowl under the leak and went to check all the other radiators in the house. She went upstairs and checked Timothy's room. She checked the radiator, but then lingered. Whenever she went into his room she would make herself remember him. His smell. The sound of his voice. The feel of his hair. His Mummy hugs. His tantrums. His Bear.

Next she checked Jake's room. A typical boy. She could see she would need a good hour in his room later. Then she went into Emma's room. Emma had got to that difficult age; crossing over from childhood to adulthood wasn't easy. Christine remembered herself as a teenager. Emma was usually quite tidy. On the top of a chest of drawers all but one of her teddies were carefully arranged. Her favourite always sat on the bed. On the top of her bookcase her collection of porcelain dolls given by her grandma were set up. They were dressed in their best clothes. It looked like the sort of display you would see in a shop window. Her dressing table was littered with the tools of her age. Lash curlers, hair straighteners, hair curlers, hair dryer, hair spray. Hair extensions ready curled and hung in a neat row. Bottles of nail varnish, lipsticks and all the other 'necessities'.

There were a couple of celebrity posters on one wall. On the other wall she still had her Beatrix Potter clock and an embroidered picture of Jemima Puddleduck. Her bedclothes were still at the pink and fluffy stage. No sign of teenage angst there yet.

Christine checked the radiator. It seemed that it was only the one in the kitchen that was leaking. She went to phone for a plumber. Amazingly one of the numbers she tried answered with a voice, not just an answer machine. More amazingly, he promised to come that afternoon.

The plumber arrived at half past two. He seemed a very nice young man. He was polite and only wanted one sugar in his coffee. He apologised that the water had to be turned off, then got on with the job. Christine would have to leave him in the house while she fetched the boys from school. She would take her handbag with her, but she locked the dining room where she kept cheque books and important papers. If anything else went missing it would be obvious.

Nothing happened. She arrived back with the boys. The plumber was still doing battle with pieces of copper piping. The water had been turned back on. Christine put the kettle on for a pot of tea.

*

Emma and Sarah strolled out of school. They were having a giggle about the deputy head. He had been threatening them all with dire consequences if they got poor results in their mock GCSEs. It was all a bit over the top. Everyone knew it was a practice run for the real thing. They all knew how important they would be. Emma and Sarah both needed good grades to do the A levels of their choice. They were hoping to get onto the same courses at the Sixth Form College so they could travel in together.

"Did you hear about Nick?" asked Sarah.

"No, but you're going to tell me," responded Emma in anticipation.

"His parents caught him doing coke and they've kicked him out. He's sofa surfing. He's at Andy's at the moment. Andy's mum is really kind; they've only got a small house and Andy's dad is out of work at the moment. You'd think Nick would have more sense. I thought he wanted to do forensics or something." Feeling uncomfortable, Emma changed the subject.

Instead they discussed the latest celebrity gossip: who was dating who; the latest scandal on TV; the model who had died of an eating disorder. When they reached Sarah's house, they agreed to meet up later after tea. They planned to do some revision together. Sarah helped Emma with her science and Emma helped Sarah remember her quotes for English Lit. This method usually worked for them and they had a good gossip as well.

Emma opened the front door. She was humming a tune and looking forward to having a cup of tea. She didn't see the tool box. Her foot caught the corner. She twisted as she fell. Her arms were trapped by the school bag. She couldn't protect herself. Her face was going to hit the corner of the radiator. It didn't happen.

At what seemed like the last millisecond she was caught by a strong arm. She was lifted onto her feet. Her bag was taken from her. Then she was gently lifted over the tools to safety. Emma looked into the face of her rescuer. He was a good-looking young man. His eyes seemed to be laughing at her. Shock and embarrassment welling up inside, she burst into tears. Then she fled to her room.

*

London

When their plates were completely empty, Simon and Tim got up to leave. Tim gave Maggie a hug and thanked her for the breakfast. She seemed to like that. No one had introduced them. She probably still didn't know Tim's name. Tim had noticed Simon call her Maggie once when they were leaving.

Tim followed Simon out the door and looked back. Kelly was getting up to follow them out. She still looked terrible. Tim didn't ask any questions. Neither did Simon. They just stood and waited for her. Once outside Kelly put her hands up to her face and winced. "I'd better get back. I need to put something on my face," she muttered. Tim noticed that her hands were shaking. She wasn't at all well.

"Should we come with you?" asked Tim, "in case that man comes back."

"I'll be OK thanks. I just need to get back to work. Maybe I'll see you around. Thanks for breakfast."

Kelly began walking away. After a few metres she turned and gave them a small wave. Tim thought it was a sad wave. He looked up at Simon. He looked sad too.

"She shouldn't have been on her own, should she," observed Tim. "You said I should always have a friend with me on the streets."

Simon nodded. They walked in silence for a while.

"D'you think she'll be alright?" asked Tim. He kept remembering the sound of her cries. Simon didn't answer. "I liked her. She was funny. She was wearing silly clothes. She didn't even have a warm coat... or a hat." Simon still didn't answer. Tim decided to change the subject.

"Where are we going today?"

"To one of my favourite freebies."

Tim saw Simon smile and was satisfied. Tim hoped it wasn't too far. He didn't really like all this walking.

Part Three

Birmingham

When Paul had joined the accountancy firm he had felt pretty secure. It wasn't the sort of job where people were made redundant. People always needed an accountant. You only got the sack if you made a mistake that lost the company money. But now with the banks going under things had changed. Many of Paul's clients were small businesses. They were struggling. Only last week the bank had foreclosed on a small company. Fifty people had lost their jobs and Paul's company had lost a valued client.

Today Paul was having a meeting with one of his oldest clients. Normally they would be having a nice lunch together somewhere in the city centre. Today they were meeting over coffee. It was a sign of the times. Paul was mulling over a problem, trying to think of a way to save Bob's company some money.

"I saw your wife on TV the other night," Bob suddenly announced.

Paul was thrown into momentary confusion. It was an area of his life that he had tried to block out. He had loved Timothy just as much as Christine did. But he had tried all these years to be strong for her. When she could no longer work, he worked harder. He got promoted. He felt it was his responsibility to make sure the rest of the family were secure. He made sure he could look after them. Bob had touched a raw nerve.

Paul pulled himself together.

"It was worth a shot," he replied, "but there has been no

response."

"I suppose you tried all the children's homes in the area," said Bob.

"We left that to the police six years ago. They all seemed to know what they were doing."

Paul looked out of the window as the memories came back.

"Look, I know it's not any of my business, but we've known each other a long time. They could have missed something, something only his family would know. He was only three, wasn't he?"

Paul nodded.

"If you'd like, I can get my assistant to do some research for you. She has far too much time on her hands at the moment and she's good at this sort of thing. I'll get her to draw up a list of contact names, addresses and numbers of all the possible places he could have been taken to in Birmingham. How's that?"

Paul could see that Bob was pleased with himself. He began to thank him. Bob held up his hand to silence his friend. "Thank me if we come up with something."

Paul sat in silence for some time after Bob had left. He wondered about telling Christine. He decided not to. There was no point getting her hopes up at this stage. Chances are they would draw a blank.

*

London

It began to rain just as Kelly reached the terrace where her basement was. She hurried down the steps. She didn't want to get wet. She was already cold. Her body was demanding a fix. It hurt like hell.

On her way back, Kelly had made a detour to a dealer. She spent most of what she had earned last night. The dealer she went to most often worked in a video store nearby. He looked about thirty but sounded about fifteen when he spoke. His speech was mostly slurred and his eyes didn't focus. But he was always friendly and seemed to like her. Kelly guessed that he had probably become a dealer to feed his own habit. So many people did that; it wasn't difficult to get hold of. It just cost so much.

Kelly let herself in. She took the black high-heeled shoe out of the window. She locked the door. She got out a small silver bag with a black tube, several syringes and some needles. She found a spoon. She mixed the heroin with some lemon juice and water. She heated it with a cigarette lighter till it dissolved. She used the tube to get the veins on her arm to pop up. Then she shot herself full.

About an hour later there was banging on the door. Kelly staggered to the door in a stupor. Her mouth hung limp and she was dribbling. The combined effect of this with her bruised and swollen face would have shocked a normal person. Kelly opened the door. It was Carol. Carol was her Maid. Kelly was one of three girls who worked for her. She took a large cut from what they earned. Carol had seen it all before. She wasn't shocked. But she was angry.

Carol pushed Kelly back into the room. She began slapping and yelling at her at the same time. She wanted to know where she had been. Had she spent all the money? She screamed at her to put her face back together. She picked up the high-heeled shoe and slammed it back down on the window sill. Then she took the key out of the lock and went out, slamming the door behind her.

Kelly sat snivelling on the floor. The slaps across her face had reopened the wound by her mouth. A trickle of blood now mingled with dribble and tears. With her brain still in a fog she decided she'd had enough. She'd had enough of Carol. She'd had enough of the dark basement. She'd had enough of the guys with their creepy habits. She knew she had to leave.

*

Tim and Simon hurried to find shelter when the rain began. They happened to be near a church, so they hurried inside. It wasn't warm but it was dry. It was very quiet. Timothy found himself whispering.

"I hope Kelly is OK," he said, "D'you think we'll see her again?"

"London's a big place. There are millions of people here. There are thousands of girls like Kelly. I'd be very surprised if we met again," Simon whispered back.

They had a little wander around and then went to see if the rain had stopped. It had. Simon announced that they would go and see if they could get some waterproof gear for Tim.

Tim recognised the place they went to. It was the same place Simon had got the sleeping bag. Tim sat on the steps to wait. It was late afternoon and the streets were busy. People were hurrying home. Tim watched. He saw ladies totter by on high heels. Men in suits were carrying briefcases or laptops. They all had their umbrellas at the ready.

It began to rain again. Tim shuffled back up the steps to get under cover. He watched people scurrying for shelter or frantically trying to get their umbrellas up. Then Tim noticed a boy standing still behind one of the ladies doing battle with her brolly. She relaxed her grip on her handbag for a split second and it was gone. The boy had snatched it and run. He ran past Tim and disappeared behind a railing.

Then Tim noticed a black boy standing a little way off from the lady. He apparently had something tucked under his 'hoody'. He was checking over his shoulder. The lady saw him. She shouted, "Thief!" and began running and pointing. The boy had run off. A man further up the street grabbed and held him. The lady ran up shouting, "He's stolen my handbag!" The man gave him a quick search. He obviously didn't have anything. At this point the boy began shouting his innocence. He claimed that he was being picked on because he was black. The man instantly let go of him as if he had been bitten. He shrugged at the lady and walked away. The lady was left standing there turning in confused circles.

Tim had seen it all. He had watched all the moves. He thought it was a clever trick. People are always ready to blame a black boy. There was a movement near him. The real thief was sitting on the step behind him. He leaned forward and hissed in Tim's ear, "If you say anything I'll tell the law it was you." Tim shook his head.

"But I didn't see anything," he lied.

"That's right," nodded the thief. He then came and sat next to Tim. There was no sign of a bag anywhere.

A moment later the black boy joined them. He grinned at the thief. He looked pleased with himself.

"It's alright," said the thief, "he won't talk." He then introduced himself. "I'm Wayne. We don't work for anyone else. We've got our own game," he said proudly. "And this is Murphy. His real name is Eddy but of course we all call him Murphy. You can see why."

Tim couldn't see why. Then he began to introduce himself. At that moment Simon appeared on the steps. Tim looked up and smiled at him. Then he turned back to speak to the boys. They were gone.

*

Worcestershire

Emma and Sarah had been revising all afternoon. They both felt they deserved the evening off. Emma got up to leave. "I'd better get home. Mum will have dinner ready soon. She doesn't like me being late. She'll make less fuss about us going out if she's in a good mood." Emma checked she had her mobile, coat and all her books and left. It wasn't far but she was glad of her warm coat. The nights were getting really cold now and very dark. She had her torch with her. There weren't many street lights in the village, only a few near the shop. It was too early for Christmas lights... Emma thought about Christmas. She had been saving some of her allowance for presents. But she had spent more than she should on going out. She'd be spending more tonight. Perhaps she could 'pretty please' her dad. He usually gave her something if she asked.

After dinner, Emma helped clear the table. Her mum always loaded the dishwasher and cleaned up. She said otherwise the kids would have an excuse not to do their homework. Emma went and sat near her dad. He had The Financial Times in his hands, but he wasn't reading it. He seemed to be staring into space. Whatever he was thinking about was making him sad. Emma knew that look. It was Timothy. Emma didn't want to break into his thoughts. She just sat and waited. He would notice her soon. He did.

"Hello Em, how's the revision going?"

"We did loads this afternoon. Sarah thinks we've earned an evening off. Trouble is, I've run out of money."

Emma put on a mock pleading face which somehow always seemed to work. Her dad laughed indulgently and gave her a tenner. "Enjoy yourself," he said, "but not so late this time."

Emma went to her room and sent a text to Sarah. Sarah's brother Ben was always happy to give them a lift. It gave him an excuse to go into Worcester. Emma got changed and tidied her hair. She touched up her makeup and chose a pair of shoes. She wore jeans. Jeans were warmer than a mini skirt and her mum wouldn't fuss. As long as she wore smart shoes and a smart top she could still get into the clubs.

Ben parked by the river. He said it was because he didn't have to pay for parking. That meant a walk over the bridge. The girls didn't mind; the river looked beautiful at night reflecting the lights from the bridge. It was the best view of the Cathedral, which was always lit up at night. Anyway, it wasn't far to walk.

They walked up past the shops. It would have been quicker through the bus station, but Ben said it wasn't safe at night. There were a lot of people about. A large group of young men were gathered near the statue of Elgar. They were very noisy. "They look a bit high," observed Ben. Emma knew what that meant. They walked by casually, avoiding eye contact.

There was a long queue outside the club. Ben looked fed up, but Sarah and Emma were happy to stand and gossip. The queue shuffled slowly forward. Then Ben nudged Emma and pointed at the group of young men coming towards them. They were the same ones who had been making all the noise.

At first they just stood behind Ben. Then suddenly one of them pushed him violently to the ground. Ben was completely taken by surprise. He struggled to his feet. Emma had watched in horrified silence. Then Sarah had turned to see what was happening. One of the others decided it looked fun. A moment later, Sarah went flying to the ground. Emma saw them come for her and took a quick step back. She wasn't aware of the kerb behind her. Her foot slipped down off the kerb and she reeled backwards towards the road. It didn't happen.

A strong arm caught her. Emma was lifted into the air and put gently back on her feet. She looked into a familiar face. She had seen those laughing eyes before.

*

London

Wayne grew up on a council estate. It had once been a place where people chose to live. Now it was a mess. The scraps of mud that used to have grass were littered with rubbish. Boards covered broken windows. Graffiti covered dilapidated walls. Dogs and runny-nosed children ran along the pavements.

Wayne's dad was mostly out of work. His mum had left when Wayne was just six. He had started pinching things from a very young age. He found he was good at it. It wasn't long before he was arrested for burglary. He was too young to be locked up. He ran away from care homes. He escaped from custody, slipping his small hands through the handcuffs. Playing was for other boys. Wayne's only game was to take on the police. He would steal hundreds of pounds and give it away, trying to buy friends. By the time he was ten, stealing was the only game he knew. He stopped going home to avoid the police. He began a life on the streets.

Then he met Murphy. Murphy's story wasn't much different. He was escaping a life of poverty and abuse. They worked out their clever scam and it paid off. Most nights they had enough to buy a good meal and a bed for the night. But there were plenty of nights when they slept rough. Wayne couldn't understand why it always seemed to rain on those nights.

Murphy was Wayne's first real friend. He never said much. He let Wayne make all the decisions. That made Wayne feel like the boss. Sometimes he wished he didn't have to do all the thinking. Sometimes he felt too tired. Sometimes he wished he had a mum to look after him. Sometimes he wished he had a room of his own. Sometimes... but not often. Mostly he was proud of himself.

Wayne and Murphy sat in a MacDonald's. They had ordered a huge meal with large fries and a large coke. They reckoned the lady must have just been to a cash point. Her purse had been stuffed full of notes. It would keep them going for a while. Wayne had the rest of the money packed evenly into his shoes. It wouldn't matter if he had his own pockets picked.

Later they went to the nearest tube station. They bought tickets. It was usually warm on the trains. They rode for a while on the Circle Line. After a while they decided to head for Leicester Square. It was evening and people would be coming to buy tickets for the movies or the theatres with money in their pockets. There would be rich pickings.

They went to work straight away. Wayne quickly picked out a victim. He grabbed her bag and Murphy created a scene. But someone else had been watching. Wayne rounded a corner and found himself grabbed by the throat. He was swung around facing away from his assailant. He could feel the steely arms gripping him. He could hear the voice. "You don't wanna see my face, man, or I'll have to use my blade." With one arm still gripping Wayne, the other took the bag. Wayne heard the swish of a flick knife opening and froze. His assailant pushed him up against the wall. He pushed his face into the brick and hissed into his ear.

"You turn around and you're dead man." Wayne believed him. He didn't move. When Murphy got there, Wayne still hadn't moved. Murphy guessed what had happened. It was part of the game. Wayne shrugged his shoulders. "He didn't take my shoes off. We'll still get a bed for the night."

*

The rain had stopped by the morning. The sun was trying to shine through the thick London air. It wasn't a 'Maggie morning'. They'd be having breakfast somewhere else today. Simon seemed to be in a good mood. He was humming and walking in long strides. Tim had to work hard to keep up. Simon checked over his shoulder making sure Tim was still there. As he did so a courier on a motorbike pulled out from a narrow alley. Simon stepped straight into his path. Tim watched the collision. As he ran up he saw the courier pulling his bike upright. He was shouting at Simon.

"You stupid, filthy old tramp, get out o' my way."

He got back on his bike and shot off. Simon was still crumpled on the ground. "Are you OK?" asked Tim anxiously. It was a silly question.

"Can you stand up? Where does it hurt?"

These sensible questions came from a man who had stopped to help. By way of an answer Simon pulled up his trouser leg. He had a very nasty gash on his shin. It seemed to Tim to go from his ankle almost to his knee. It must have been very deep. There was a lot of blood.

The man moved quickly. He used Simon's trousers to cover the wound back up. He pulled the fabric tightly across and ordered Tim to hold it in place. He whipped out his mobile and called for an ambulance. Simon was looking very pale. Tim found himself crying. The man crouched down next to Tim.

"It's OK, an ambulance will be here soon. I'll come to Casualty with you. Can you tell me the gentleman's name?"

"Simon," sniffed Tim.

"And you are?"

"His son," lied Tim. He thought it would be safer. They'd ask fewer questions.

"My name is Martin," said the man. He didn't think that Tim looked as if he could be any relation to Simon. "I don't think you are telling me the whole truth," he said, "but don't worry, I'll cover for you. You can tell me all about it while we're waiting. Have you ever been to Casualty before?" Tim shook his head. "Well I warn you it will feel as if you're waiting forever." Martin put a comforting arm around Tim's shoulder. "He'll be OK, just stitches and antibiotics I expect."

The ambulance arrived, Simon was lifted in and Tim and Martin clambered in after him. One of the paramedics began to sterilise and dress the wound en route. Simon was looking anxious. Martin leaned across, "I'll take care of the boy, relax." Simon now saw the white dog collar around Martin's neck. He started to breathe more easily. "Thanks," he said weakly.

It was a long wait at Casualty. They asked a lot of questions and wanted all sorts of details. Martin took over and sorted it all out. Tim wondered what he could have told them. All he knew was Simon's first name. After a very long wait, Simon was taken through for his stitches. He would have to have antibiotic injections to stop any infections, otherwise the wound wouldn't heal. Martin took Tim to get a drink. Simon had to bear it on his own. When it was all over, the nurse came out to talk to Martin.

"He needs to keep the weight off his leg for at least a week. He needs these antibiotics four times a day. If there's any sign of infection, just bring him straight back here." She smiled at Martin and went to get Simon. He was on crutches and looked very sorry for himself.

Martin had ordered a taxi to take them all back to where he lived. As they drove along the sun was still shining. Tim realised that they hadn't even had breakfast yet. He had no idea where they were going.

*

Kelly packed a small bag with her things. She didn't have much. That was OK; there would be less to carry. She sat on the edge of the bed and wondered what to do next. It was all very well to pack her bag and decide to leave, but where would she go? Kelly knew she couldn't go back to her family. She had to work. She needed money. She had no qualifications. Anyway, other jobs didn't pay enough. She didn't know any other way of life.

If she left London, where would she go? It would be the same work but she wouldn't know her way around. She'd probably be safer in London. She didn't have any friends. The other two girls who worked for Carol were already friends before Kelly arrived. Kelly was still 'the new one'.

The only other person she knew was Dave, her dealer. He might let her sleep on a sofa if she gave him some of her earnings. She was used to paying for her keep. At least he wouldn't slap and scream at her like Carol. Kelly pushed her bag under the bed out of sight. She'd find out first if Dave would put her up somewhere. She wasn't going to make herself homeless. There was no way she wanted to sleep rough like Tim and the tramp. At least she had a roof over her head and a bed to lie on.

At first Dave wanted nothing to do with Kelly. He said he was already sharing his crummy flat with a mate. But she persuaded him to change his mind. He liked the sound of the extra money. They arranged to meet up later. Kelly felt pleased with herself. Dave's flat wasn't too far away. She would still know her way around. She would be her own boss. She'd be able to pick up plenty of clients around Paddington Station. There would be competition from the other girls, but even though she would be sixteen next week she still looked very young. The guys seemed to like it.

41

Martin opened the front door and then turned to help Simon up the step. The house was an ordinary Victorian brick terrace. There was a sign on the door saying 'The Manse'. Tim thought it was a silly name for a house. They stepped into the hallway. The floor still had the geometric Victorian tiles. The ceiling was high and made their footsteps echo. Martin showed them into a square room. It had a high ceiling, tall windows and a wooden floor. One wall was completely covered by books. The shelves went all the way up to the ceiling. There was a big desk covered in papers in front of the window. There were two big old-fashioned wing armchairs. They looked very worn and lumpy. There was also a round wicker chair with a fluffy cushion. Tim sat on this. Martin helped Simon into one of the big armchairs.

"I'll just go and put the kettle on for a pot of tea, and I'll see if I have any biscuits." Martin smiled at Tim as he went out of the room.

"It's a bit old and spooky," said Tim softly, "d'you think it's haunted?"

"I think we've been very lucky. He's a very kind man, so you be nice to him," replied Simon.

Tim got up and looked at the books. They looked old and tatty and boring.

"D'you think he has read all these books?" asked Tim. Simon looked up at the shelves, "They look as if they have been read lots of times."

Martin came in with the tea and biscuits. Tim forgot about the books. "So Tim, where are you from?" asked Martin.

Tim knew Martin didn't believe he was Simon's son. He gave him a more familiar story. He told about a mother who had been an actress. He told about a father who was in business and drove a Porsche. He said how proud he was of his brother Carl who was training to become a pro-footballer. He spoke about a house in Birmingham and a villa in Spain. Then he added a bit to bring it up to date. "My aunt gave me a lift down to

London to visit my brother. She dropped me at East Croydon station and I caught a train to Victoria. Carl was supposed to meet me but he didn't show up. Then I met Simon."

Tim looked across at Simon and saw the disbelief in his face. Then he looked up at Martin. Martin just smiled at him. He offered Tim another biscuit. When the biscuit had gone Martin looked deep into Tim's eyes. "Now tell me the real story. I won't do anything you don't want me to. You can trust me." Tim looked back into Martin's eyes. They were dark and deep and gentle. Tim knew he could trust him. He glanced across at Simon who nodded encouragingly. Tim wanted to speak, but he didn't know what to say. He had told so many lies about himself over the years. He had stopped himself thinking about his real family. He knew it would make him cry if he began now. "I can't remember," Tim whispered, hoping not to have to say any more.

"What part of your story do you know?" Martin asked quietly.

"Bear, I know about Bear." Tim reached into his rucksack and pulled out a scruffy old bear with beady eyes.

"My Mummy gave him to me." And Tim wept.

Part Four

Birmingham

Paul was tired and despondent. He had tried about two thirds of the places on Bob's list. There had been one or two boys called Timothy. They all had a different surname and were the wrong age anyway. He didn't like keeping things from Christine, either. It made him feel uncomfortable, even though he still felt it was for the best.

The next home on his list was south of the centre. It would be easy to call in on the way home from work. If he left the office fifteen minutes early he would get home at roughly the usual time. His secretary had rung in advance and made an appointment with someone who would have access to records.

Paul looked for somewhere to park and then found the main entrance. He went through all the usual security and ID checks and was allowed in. He was introduced to a Mrs Griffiths. She had seen the TV show. After receiving their phone call earlier that day she had already done some research. "I've gone through all the records for the last six years. There's no mention of anyone by that name. We did have a Tim who would have been the same age, but his name wasn't Whittaker. I am sorry." She looked genuinely sorry for him. Mrs Griffiths did care about the boys here. She knew about some of the things that went on that shouldn't. But without creating a prison environment it was almost impossible to prevent it. She did her best.

"What was his name?" Paul asked idly.

"Timothy Brum," she replied.

"What a strange name," Paul said, a puzzled look on his face.

"Yes, I suppose it is. I've never really thought about it."

Paul began walking away. There was something nagging at the back of his mind. It was something Bob had said, "something only his family would know." Paul stood still a moment and closed his eyes. He tried to picture Timothy as he had last seen him. He tried to remember his voice. In his mind he heard Timothy trying to say his name... Paul almost ran back to the startled Mrs Griffiths. He found himself shouting. "What was his middle name, did he have a middle name?"

Mrs Griffiths didn't know; she would have to look it up. She went to the computer. Paul could feel his heart pounding with excitement. Eventually she spoke. "Yes... Nathaniel."

Paul felt his emotions explode in his head. "That's him!" he began shouting, "That's him!"

Mrs Griffiths was speechless. She stood staring at Paul as he danced a jig around the office. "Tell me," Paul said when he had calmed down a bit, "do you remember if he had a bear?"

Mrs Griffiths began to feel very strange. Yes, she remembered that bear very clearly. It had caused a lot of trouble. How was she going to tell this man that they had lost his son? "Yes," she said, "he had a teddy bear. I think I had better call my superior to have a chat with you."

Paul sat in his car and wept. He had found and lost his son again all in the same day. He couldn't drive just yet. It wouldn't be safe. He couldn't tell Christine. She would be utterly devastated. He needed to tell someone. He picked up his mobile and rang Bob. Paul managed to control his voice long enough to explain to Bob what he had discovered.

"When did this happen?" asked Bob.

"A few weeks ago," Paul managed to answer.

"Look, don't despair. You know he's alive. That's fantastic news. You'll find him. Will you let my assistant do some more research? I can get her to find all the charities that help with runaways or people sleeping rough in Birmingham. Pull yourself together man, we'll find him." On this positive note Bob hung up.

Paul called into a café on the way home. He bought a cup of tea and gave himself time to calm down. He looked around him. "He could be anywhere," he thought to himself. "At least he's alive… and he still has Bear."

*

London

Tim clutched the five-pound note tightly in his hand. In his other hand he held a small carrier bag containing a package and a few letters. Martin had asked him to walk to the post office. Martin needed to help Simon have a wash, as he wasn't supposed to get the dressing on his leg wet. Tim was happy to have a reason to go out. Martin had given him detailed directions. It wasn't difficult to find. There wasn't much of a queue and within a few minutes, Tim was back outside. There was some change and Tim pushed it deep into his pocket.

On the way, Tim had passed a few shops. He decided to take his time going back. It was a cold morning towards the end of November. Tim watched his breath come out in clouds. He peered in at the windows. Inside the shops looked warm and bright. Christmas shopping was already in full swing in the city. There were decorated Christmas trees and coloured lights. Tim wondered what Simon did for Christmas. Tim had never enjoyed it. The only presents he ever got were cheap gestures from staff. He supposed that was better than nothing, but somehow they never really felt as if they were his own. Somehow they always felt as if they were on loan and he would have to give them back one day.

In one window there was a whole winter scene with a Santa and reindeer. There were garden gnomes with boxes wrapped as presents next to them. Tim guessed they were meant to be Santa's elves. There was a bird table with some fake robins standing on the top. Someone had put other garden ornaments into the scene. Tim thought it looked stupid. He strolled on past a fashion boutique with tinsel draped over everything and flashing blue lights round the window.

The next shop that he bothered to look at was very small. It looked as if they sold art and craft materials. Someone had made a beautiful tiny nativity scene for the window. Tim found himself gazing at it for a long time. If you looked carefully you could spot all the tiny details. There was a miniature bird perched on the corner of the manger. Joseph had a tiny lamb tucked under his arm. The baby's chubby arms were stretched out towards Mary. He could even see little white doves up in the rafters of the stable. Tim tried to imagine himself into the scene to be with that family in that wonderful place.

Tim was brought rudely back to reality as a man bumped into him. Tim was knocked completely off balance. He tried to save himself, putting his hand out towards the wall. His hand scraped down the brickwork as he fell. The man didn't apologise or even stop. Tim stood up and brushed himself down. He looked at his hand. The graze was deep. There was grit in it and it was bleeding. It would need cleaning when he got back to Martin's house. Tim was angry and determined not to let anyone see that he was hurt.

Now Tim walked quickly. He wished he could catch up with that man and give him a good kick. His hand had begun to throb and it was stinging. He was glad they were staying with Martin. Martin would have something to put on it. He might even get the biscuits out. Tim rang the doorbell. Martin opened the door. Tim just held up his hand for Martin to see. Tim had been right. Martin took him through to the kitchen. He gently bathed the graze and then put some soothing antiseptic cream on. He found a large plaster that just covered it. Next the kettle was switched on for a pot of tea and the biscuit tin was lifted down from the cupboard.

"Did you find the post office OK?" asked Martin.

"Yes. Your change is in my pocket."

Tim dug his hand deep into his pocket and pulled out...

nothing!

"I didn't pinch it!" he yelled in a panic.

"It's alright," said Martin reassuringly, "I expect the man who knocked you down took it. That's how they work. I don't suppose he got much for his trouble, did he?"

"It was nearly two pounds," muttered Tim. Martin might not think it was much, but Tim and Simon could make it go a long way. If Martin didn't want the money he could have told him to spend it. He could have bought some sweets. Tim's hand was throbbing again and he felt miserable. "Can I have another biscuit please?"

*

Worcester

It was Saturday. There were crowds of shoppers in Worcester. This Saturday was especially busy because of the Victorian Market. People were arriving by the coachload. Some roads had been closed for the fairground rides. There were German food stalls, chestnut stalls and craft stalls. You could buy recycled cans made into works of art. There were hats galore and mulled wine. There was even an old man in a top hat playing a hurdy-gurdy. Emma always found it especially exciting because it meant her birthday was near.

Emma and Sarah sat eating pizza. They had managed to find two seats by the window. Emma had a notepad in front of her. She was making a list of friends to invite to her party. They would be going to the cinema. A new *Bond* movie had just been released. Afterwards, they planned to go for a pizza. Emma's mum had agreed to pay for the food so long as she didn't invite more than ten friends. The difficulty for Emma was who *not* to invite.

Glancing out of the window, Emma caught sight of a familiar face. It was their friendly plumber, Luke. She waved, half expecting him not to see her. He waved back. Then he stopped to make a call on his mobile. Emma felt herself blushing as she realised that he was coming in.

"You've gone bright red," stated Sarah unhelpfully.

"It's Luke, he's coming in here," Emma hissed back at her.

Emma gave herself a mental look-over. She smoothed down her hair then grabbed a serviette to wipe around her mouth.

"He must like you," whispered Sarah.

Emma shushed Sarah and turned to watch as Luke approached.

"I have to go to the ladies," announced Sarah, getting up as she spoke.

Luke sat in her chair. "Christmas shopping?" he asked.

"We came down for the fair and we're planning my birthday." Emma decided to be bold. "I don't suppose you're free Friday night, are you? We're going to see the new Bond movie and coming here afterwards."

Emma held her breath as a slow smile spread across Luke's face. "Cool! Yeah, I can make it. What time?"

Sarah dawdled as long as she could in the ladies. By the time she got back to the table Luke had gone. Emma sat staring out of the window, a stupid grin on her face.

"Well?" asked Sarah.

"He's coming on Friday. What am I going to wear?"

*

London

Kelly celebrated her sixteenth birthday by learning a new trade. She began working in a massage parlour to get some extra cash. By now she was using anything she could get: heroin, cocaine, crack, pills, ex, weed. She worked hard to pay for it. The rent Dave charged for sleeping on his grotty settee wasn't cheap either. There was a hotel nearby where the manager looked the other way when the working girls took their clients in. He didn't charge much for his rooms. Neither did he spend much on their maintenance. Everything was sticky: the walls, the carpet, the curtains, the door handles. At least here Kelly was her own boss.

During the day she crashed out at Dave's. The settee was only just long enough to sleep on. It was lumpy and had dark stains on the cushions. It smelled of a mixture of fish and cigarette smoke. Dave had given her an old quilt. It stank but at least it was warm. There was a battered chest of drawers where she could keep a few things. The bathroom was tiny but there was a mirror, so she could do her makeup. There was a kitchen-ette, which no one ever seemed to use. Kelly mostly ate out, picking up a burger or chips between clients.

Kelly was tired. She had worked hard all night. She was desperate for a fix. She climbed the dark narrow back stairway to Dave's flat. Inside she could see Dave and his flat mate crashed out on the double bed. Dave should have been at work by now. She went over and gave him a shove. "Hey, wake up; you'll lose your job if you're late again." Dave groaned but made himself get up. Kelly heard him dress and go out. She cooked up some heroin and took her fix.

At six o'clock Dave got back from work. He slammed the door shut. Kelly woke up. She slowly sat up and watched Dave go over to the bed. His flat mate was still there. Dave went and looked at him. "Hey, I don't think he's breathing."

Kelly staggered to her feet. She could see straight away there was something wrong. His lips were blue. She touched his face. It was stone cold. "He's dead. You'd better call the police." It wasn't the first time Kelly had seen someone overdose. It was just part of life. She hadn't known him. He hadn't been interested in her. She went into the bathroom and peered into the mirror. It was going to take a lot of makeup to get her face ready for work tonight.

*

51

Simon woke up. It was half past five. It was very dark outside. At least he could get up and walk around a bit now. His leg was nearly completely healed. At first Simon had found the long wait until breakfast interminable. Martin had made the settee in his study into a bed so he didn't have to climb the stairs. Simon got up and switched on the light. He ran his eyes over the books on the shelves. Before his troubles, when he had taken his family on holiday, he used to buy novels. It was nearly always by Dick Francis, the former jockey. He had read his first one at secondary school and enjoyed it. He had never bothered trying other authors. Martin's shelves had very few novels. He found some by C S Lewis. There were some old science fiction novels by Isaac Asimov. There were a lot of autobiographies. Most of his books were theology or philosophy. One book caught his eye. It was the title that intrigued him, *The Heavenly Man*. Simon laughed to himself. That was how he thought of Martin.

Simon went over to the window to draw back the curtains. It was still dark but there was plenty of bustle out there to watch. He was enjoying the comfort of Martin's home, but he missed his freedom. He missed his friends. Maggie would be worried. He even missed the boy. Tim slept upstairs somewhere. He got up late and went to bed early. Simon knew it was better for him, but he missed his company.

Turning away from the window Simon brushed a sheet of paper from Martin's desk. He bent down and picked it up. He didn't mean to look at it but his eye was caught by the word Tim. He found himself reading. There were some telephone numbers. Mostly they were London numbers. A few were 0121 numbers, which he knew were Birmingham. Martin had written some notes. Simon read '...has a Birmingham accent.' Simon realised that Martin must have been making phone calls about Tim. He was very angry. How dare this person who was supposed to be so caring go behind his back? How dare he try to take Tim away from him? Furiously, he tore the paper into tiny pieces. He threw them into the wastepaper basket. He flung himself into an armchair, anger welling up inside.

There was nothing Simon could do yet. He would have to wait for Tim to get up. He sat in angry silence. After a few minutes he heard a little voice in his own head.

"How dare you keep Tim away from his family?"

"He hasn't got one!" he shouted back at himself.

"How do you know?" came back the annoying voice.

"They'll just send him back to where he ran away from," Simon muttered to himself.

He sat alone in silence waiting for the others to get up. He pictured Martin's face. He was a good man... a heavenly man. He knew really that Martin would only do what he believed was right for Tim. But Tim didn't want to go back. Simon knew that. Simon didn't want to upset Martin after all his kindness, but it was time for them to leave.

*

Tim woke up slowly. Light filtered through the curtains. His bed was warm and soft. It smelled of Martin, sort of lemony. He pushed back the deep duvet. He swung his legs around and sat up. He dug his toes into the carpet. He had never slept in a room with carpet before. He enjoyed the luxury. He was keeping his few belongings on an old dressing table. Along one wall was a built-in wardrobe. Tim had peeked in there when he first arrived. It was full of boxes of family photographs and yet more books. There were some suits on hangers and boxes of old Christmas cards.

Martin had lent Tim an old shirt to sleep in. He took it off and got dressed. He went to the bathroom. He was already hungry and wondered what was for breakfast. He checked Bear was safely tucked into his bag and then went downstairs. In the large Victorian kitchen he found Martin and Simon waiting for him. Martin smiled at him.

"How many sausages this morning?" he asked.

Tim felt as if he could eat half a dozen.

"Two please."

He sat down at the big square table. Martin passed him a mug of hot tea. Simon hadn't spoken. He was staring into his mug of tea. He was frowning. Tim sipped his tea.

"You alright?" Tim asked.

Simon nodded, but he was still frowning. He looked as if he was trying to work something out. As if he was trying to do some difficult mental arithmetic. Tim sipped his tea again. He knew Simon was worried. Martin put a plate of sausages, egg and toast in front of Tim. Tim focused his attention on his breakfast.

Tim finished his last mouthful. Martin pulled up a chair and sat down next to him.

"You have a Birmingham accent," he said, "have you lived there long?"

Tim was caught by surprise. "Yes, nearly all my life, I..." he hesitated and tried to think back. What had he already told Martin? "I told you before that my parents have a house in Birmingham and a villa in Spain."

Martin looked sad and disappointed. Tim wanted to be able to tell him the truth. He dared not. He wasn't going back to that place. No one could make him go back.

Simon stood up. He was still frowning. "Tim, go and get your things," he ordered. "We're very grateful for everything you've done for us Martin, but it's time for us to go."

Tim was shocked. He hadn't liked Martin's question but he liked staying with him. He thought Simon was happy there. Simon looked cross and told Tim to get a move on.

Tim ran upstairs to get his things. He felt confused. He didn't want to go, but Simon was his friend, his new family. He pushed Bear down, well into the bag. He gave a last look around the warm bedroom. He went downstairs to Simon.

Simon was already waiting by the front door. He must have packed up his things before breakfast. Martin handed Simon a piece of paper. "If you change your mind and want to come back, this is the address and phone number. You can call me any time." A muffled "Thank you" came from somewhere under

54

Simon's beard. The door was opened. Tim and Simon stepped out onto the street. A wall of cold air hit them. Simon strode away. Tim took a deep breath and chased after him.

*

Wayne and Murphy sat shivering on a bench. They were in Hyde Park. Not for any particular reason except that here they could sit legally. Here they could relax for a while. At least they could if it weren't so cold. The weather had suddenly changed. An icy wind seemed to blow right through their clothes. They hadn't had much luck the last few days. No one seemed to be carrying any cash. It was all credit cards. Wayne could only get peanuts in exchange for them. Not enough to live on.

"Listen Murph, we're not g'nna make it. It's too cold. We need to come up with a new game, fast." Murphy just nodded as he shivered in his thin clothes. "We might 'ave to go an' work at Paddington with the girls," Wayne continued. A look of sheer horror spread over Murphy's face. He shook his head violently.

"No way!" he shouted.

Wayne knew that would be a last resort. He would have to go it alone if it came to it.

"Help me think, then. Where can we get our hands on some cash?"

"A bank?" offered Murphy.

"Too much security," sighed Wayne. But it set off a train of thought. He began to think about all the places that had security guards. Slowly a plan began to evolve in his imagination.

Forty minutes later, Murphy knew his lines. They agreed to meet back at the same bench later. Their first target was a hardware store. Wayne needed a screwdriver. Their usual role-play worked. Murphy created the diversion and Wayne sauntered out, screwdriver in hand. Their next target was a pharmacy. Here they 'collected' shaving foam.

Half an hour later they were in the foyer of a museum.. Wayne didn't know what exhibits they had in there. But he knew it had a donation box. He had watched people putting in their cash. He nodded at Murphy, who went into the gents. Wayne stood near the donation box. He kept looking at his watch and at the door. He looked as if he was waiting to meet someone who was late. Moments later Murphy ran out of the gents foaming at the mouth. He flung himself to the floor. He thrashed his arms about and kicked his legs. He made terrible gurgling noises. A crowd quickly formed. Someone shouted something about an epileptic fit. The security guards went to take charge. Someone else was shouting about spoons for his mouth. The security guards ordered the crowds to stand back. They took control of the situation.

Wayne took out the screwdriver. He opened the donation box. He stuffed the notes into his pocket. It took about fifteen seconds. His image was caught on CCTV. But he was gone before anyone noticed. He knew the police would recognise him. But he also knew they would never find him.

A couple of hours later, they were back at the park bench. Wayne had picked up a burger meal on his way. They would be warm tonight. Tomorrow they would work an art gallery.

*

The phone rang in Martin's study. Martin strode down the hallway, hoping that it would be Simon.

"Hello? Is that Martin Allen?" It was a woman's voice. Martin was disappointed. He had been cross with himself all morning. He should have done more to help Tim. A boy of that age should be in a warm, loving home. By law he should be going to school. He tried to focus his thoughts on the phone call.

"Yes, how can I help?" he asked.

"My name is Melanie Griffiths. I understand that you have been making enquiries about a boy called Tim from Birmingham?"

She had Martin's full attention now. "Yes, what can you tell me?" he asked eagerly.

56

Mrs Griffiths explained that Tim had run away some weeks ago. She told Martin about the arrival of Mr Whittaker and how they had discovered that the Whittakers were Tim's long lost family. She told Martin how devastated Mr Whittaker had been when she had to tell him that Tim had run away. "Have you found him?" she asked.

Sadly Martin explained how Tim had been staying with him for a week and had left just that morning. "The old man he's with does have my card. We'll have to pray that he gets in touch." Martin tried to reassure Mrs Griffiths.

"Just one more thing, did he have an old teddy bear?" she asked.

*

Simon had brought Tim back to the basement for the night. It was the same place that they had found Kelly. Tonight it was much colder. Tim had got used to a warm room. He thought about the soft carpet. He thought about sausages and hot tea for breakfast. He thought about Martin. He missed him.

Tim snuggled down into his sleeping bag. He tried to sleep. Simon was already snoring. It was no good. He was too cold. It was his feet that wouldn't warm up. He kept thinking about food. They had been given some hot soup late that evening. But it wasn't enough. As he lay there he heard a car pull up. He listened in the dark and wondered if Kelly had come back. He heard the same noises as before. This time he would go and look sooner. Maybe he could stop the man from hitting her.

Tim crawled out of his sleeping bag. He crept along the ground on all fours. He hardly dared breathe. He didn't want to make any sound at all. As he rounded a pillar they came into view. Tim saw straight away that it wasn't Kelly. But the girl was very young.

Tim tucked himself back into the shadows. He waited for the sounds to stop. The girl was making no sound now. Tim cautiously looked under the bumper of a parked car. He got a full view of the man's face. It was vaguely familiar. He must have seen him before. But he hadn't seen his face last time. Tim drew back into the shadows again and waited.

After a few minutes he heard the car drive away. He waited a few more minutes and then crept out. Tim wondered if this girl would need somewhere to sleep. It would be warmer with two in his sleeping bag. She still made no sound. Tim walked softly up to her so as not to startle her. "Hey," he whispered, "are you OK?" She didn't respond. Tim supposed that she hadn't heard. He put his hand on her shoulder and gave her a gentle shove. "Hey, d'you need any help?" He spoke louder this time.

But the girl just toppled sideways onto the ground. She stared up at him with unblinking eyes. He now realised that she wasn't breathing. Tim jumped up and ran back towards Simon.

"Simon, I think she's dead!" he shouted in Simon's ear.

Simon sat bolt upright. "What are you shouting about?"

"It's the girl over there… I think she's dead," sobbed Tim.

Tim found himself crying. He couldn't stop. He was shaking too. Simon squeezed himself out of the sleeping bag and strode over to where Tim was pointing. He knelt down and checked for signs of life.

"We can't help her now. Did you see who did this?"

Tim nodded.

"Did he see you?"

Tim shook his head.

Simon wasted no more time. He packed up their things. For a change he carried Tim's bag as well. He took hold of Tim's hand and dragged him from the basement as fast as he could go. Neither spoke. Tim was still shaking. Tim was sick.

They spent the rest of the night huddled in the doorway of a shop. Tim slept a bit. He began to think running away had been a mistake.

Part Five

London

Simon was shaking Tim. Tim was annoyed. He felt as if he had only just dropped off to sleep.

"I'm sorry to wake you up, but we can't stay here any longer. It isn't safe." Simon stuffed some cardboard back into his bag. He had been sitting on it. He made Tim stand up and packed away his bed. They didn't have much to carry. They were both wearing every single item of clothing they had. Tim couldn't have done much by himself. His hands were so cold that his fingers wouldn't move. He was very tired. His clothes still smelled of sick from last night.

"It must be a Maggie morning," announced Simon, "I think we need a good breakfast." He was obviously making an effort to sound cheerful. "I bet she wondered where we were last week. I never miss my Maggie mornings."

Again Simon picked up both bags. Tim was grateful. He looked up into Simon's big hairy face. "Thanks," he said, "for, you know, looking after me and showing me around." Simon looked embarrassed. He scratched behind his ear and looked as if he wanted to say something. Then he shrugged. "Let's go," he said and strode away. Tim stuffed his hands in his pockets. Then he hurried after Simon.

It was still very dark. They stepped over the legs of other people still huddled in their doorways. Tim nearly fell over a box. Inside was a bundle of clothes which shouted at him to "Clear off!" Tim just wanted to sit down and go back to sleep. Simon kept encouraging him on. "C'mon, it's not far now. Think about those sausages. It'll be warm inside."

They arrived at the bakery. It was completely dark. There was no sign of life. Not a single light on. Simon knocked on the door. He didn't expect it to be opened. It wasn't. Instead they sat down on the doorstep and waited. London was waking up. Tim could hear tradesmen shouting. Doors of delivery vans slammed. Lights came on around them. Not in the bakery. Tim put his head against Simon. He drifted off to sleep. He woke sometime later to the sound of the door being unlocked. Simon helped him to his feet.

A middle-aged man they hadn't seen before opened the door. He was startled at the sight of them.

"What are you doing here?" It wasn't a friendly question.

"We're looking for Maggie."

"Oh, well you won't find her here I'm afraid." His voice was less aggressive now. "She fell over last week and broke her hip. She's in hospital. Just a minute." He hurried away. A few moments later he reappeared with a piece of paper. He handed it to Simon. "This is the name and address of the hospital and the ward she's on. She loves having visitors. She should have retired years ago, you know. She won't be allowed back to work now, though. Something to do with insurance." He looked sad. "We'll all miss her... a lovely lady. Give her my love when you see her." He nodded at them and bustled away, closing the door behind him.

Simon looked at the piece of paper. "It's a long way on foot. We can't visit today. We need breakfast before we can do anything else. C'mon." Tim set off once more chasing after Simon. He really hoped it wasn't far.

*

Simon took Tim to the Salvation Army hostel. He was sure he would be given something to eat there. He was right. As usual he was greeted with smiles and warmth. He was able to stuff a roll into his pocket to give to Tim. They gave him a bottle of water to take away. Tim was huddled on the steps outside. Simon handed him the roll and watched while he ate. Simon began to question his own motives. He knew Tim didn't want to go back to wherever he had run away from. But he also knew that he shouldn't be living on the streets. Perhaps he should take him back to Martin. If he left him there he would be Martin's responsibility.

Simon knew that he enjoyed Tim's company. His thoughts turned to Maggie. She had spent her life helping other people. He thought about the Salvation Army just giving without question. He thought about Martin offering them his home. Simon made up his mind. He would take Tim back to Martin's this evening. In the meantime, he would enjoy Tim's company for one last day. He decided to go back to the gallery. They had sat and enjoyed looking at paintings together on that first day. "C'mon," he said to Tim, "I know somewhere warm where we can go till supper time."

*

Birmingham

Paul looked at his desk diary. It was Friday. He was looking forward to the weekend. He didn't have many clients this morning. He had kept the afternoon free of appointments. He wanted time to tie up any loose ends before he went home. At the top of the page it said: 'Emma's sixteenth birthday' and 'book meal for Chris'. He picked up the phone and dialled a number. He didn't need to look it up. He had dialled this number enough times to memorise it. It was their favourite restaurant, the Masons Arms. It was just outside the village on the road into Worcester. They were always welcomed as if they were family. The waitress would bring their regular drinks to the table without needing to be asked. They always remembered just how Paul and Chris liked their meals cooked.

Paul booked a table for two for half past seven. He was planning to talk to Chris about his discoveries. He had been waiting for the right moment. He had been over the conversation many times in his head, always trying to find a way to explain things so that Chris would have hope. The trouble was, they still didn't know where Timothy was. The only good news really was that he was alive. Paul put the phone down and almost immediately it rang.

"Hello, is that Mr Whittaker?"

"Yes, can I help you?"

"It's Melanie Griffiths from the children's home. We've had some news about Tim. Now don't get too excited, we still don't know exactly where he is right now. What we *have* discovered is where he has been. Yesterday I spoke to a church minister called Martin Allen in London."

"London!" interjected Paul. "How did he get there?"

"Well, we don't know all the details yet, but apparently he stayed with the Reverend for just under a week."

"Well, where is he now?" Paul almost shouted.

"I think perhaps it would be better if you directed your questions to the Reverend yourself. Do you have pen and paper? I'll give you his number."

Paul wrote down the number. He thanked Mrs Griffiths for all her efforts and hung up. He stared at the phone number. He wasn't sure what to ask. He wasn't sure if he wanted to know "all the details", as Mrs Griffiths had put it. He would probably have to rethink what he said to Chris tonight.

Paul dialled the number. His heart had begun thumping. He could feel the adrenaline rush. No one answered. He let the phone ring. It went to answer phone. He began to speak, but then hung up. He would try again this afternoon when all his appointments were over.

*

London

Tim and Simon sat looking at one of their favourite Turner paintings. They had been sitting in silence for some time. Each was busy with his own thoughts. Tim broke the silence. "D'you think we should tell the police about what I saw?" he asked.

Simon was thoughtful for a while. "That depends on what you can tell them. Could you describe the man well enough?"

"Yes, I think so. Don't they have photographs of people that you can look through like on TV?" Tim had seen that on a detective series.

"The problem with that is they only have photos of people who already have a criminal record; people who've been caught for something before. The police will want to know all about you and they would ask questions about me." Simon could just imagine them trying to blame him because he was there.

"But we must do *something*. That man is a murderer. If no one stops him, he'll do it again. Think how bad we would feel if we found out he'd killed someone else and we could have stopped it." Tim could see the newspaper headlines in his imagination.

"You're right," agreed Simon, "but we need a plan so that we don't get into trouble ourselves."

They relapsed into silence. Then gradually they became aware of a noise. It sounded like a great crowd of people all talking at once. At first it sounded quite distant. But it was definitely getting louder and closer. Simon was curious. "Let's go and see what's going on." Down in the spacious entrance hall, a large crowd had gathered. There were a lot of people with cameras. Tim could even see what looked like TV cameras. They kept looking at the doorway expectantly. A red carpet had been laid from the door into one of the exhibition halls.

"They must be expecting a celebrity," said Simon.

"Can we go down and have a look?"

"OK, but don't get in anyone's way or we might be asked to

leave."

When they were closer, they could see posters announcing the opening of a new exhibition. Tim wanted to know who the celebrity was. He went up to a well-dressed lady carrying a note-book. She looked as if she would know something. "Excuse me, do you know who the celebrity is?" he asked politely. The lady looked down at him. She was evidently shocked at his appear-ance, but replied anyway. "It's Ross Edwards; you know, the TV presenter. He'll be here any minute. I should stand back if I were you. You might get knocked over in the stampede." She laughed, "We journalists don't let anything stand in our way." She watched Tim smile and then shooed him away.

Simon had come closer and was standing by Tim now. They were still quite close to the lady journalist. They had actually got a very good view from where they were. Suddenly there was a lot of shouting outside. They could see cameras flashing and people waving their arms. Then the doors opened and the celebrity came through. There was pandemonium in the hall. Everyone was shouting at once. For a while Tim couldn't see anything. All the flashing lights of the photographers blinded him.

Then he saw the man. He was wearing a pink satin suit with a white frilly shirt. His hair had been deliberately brushed into a mess on one side. On the other it was sculpted into an asymmetric Mohican. Tim looked at his full, flabby face and his loose, sulky mouth. He had seen that face before. "That's him!" he shouted. He looked up at Simon. "That's him, the man in the basement; he's the murderer!"

Tim opened his mouth to shout again and felt a hand firmly clapped over it. Simon had reacted quickly, but not before at least two other people had heard. The lady journalist had spun around, dictaphone at the ready. The other person to react was a man in a grey suit nearby. He was wearing dark shades and had a mobile receiver clipped to his ear. He kept his eyes on Tim while he evidently spoke to someone.

Two other pairs of eyes had been watching. Wayne and Murphy had come to the gallery to collect some cash. They had been frustrated by the crowds, but decided to hang around. Wayne thought there would be a good chance of finding cash in some of these wallets. He knew journalists always carried plenty. They had caught sight of Tim and were on their way over when they had seen his outburst. Wayne had seen the reaction of the journalist. He had also noticed the man in shades. Wayne was curious. He decided to keep an eye on the proceedings.

Simon still had his hand over Tim's mouth. He began backing away from the crowds. The lady journalist followed. Her instincts told her that there was a story here. "Hi, my name is Kate. Can I talk to you? We can go into that side room. No one else is in there. There could be some money in it for you." Tim pulled Simon's hand away. He spoke quietly now.

"I just want him caught before he kills again," he said in a pleading tone.

"Tell me what you know and I'll do my best," said Kate. She looked over her shoulder to see if anyone else was listening.

Kate led them into the furthest corner of the room. She switched on her dictaphone. She didn't waste any time.

"What's your name?" she asked.

Tim," came the short reply.

"How old are you?"

"Nine."

"When did this happen?"

"Last night."

"Where were you?"

Kate kept the questions short. Tim gave short replies and wasted no words. When he had finished his account he added, "It nearly happened before. It was a girl called Kelly. We took her to breakfast the next morning and…"

Tim was interrupted by the arrival on the scene of the man in shades. He walked quickly up to Tim and took him roughly by the arm. "I've got orders to remove you vagrants from the building. Let's go!"

Kate had hurriedly put the dictaphone in her pocket. She took out her notebook and pen and pretended to write.

"What's this vagrant been saying?" the man growled at Kate.

"He was talking about one of the paintings," she lied.

Simon chipped in: "Yes, you know, 'Millbank', by Turner." The man looked momentarily confused. Then he received a message in his ear. He dragged Tim out of the room. "I've got my orders. You too, old man."

Kate was left alone in the room. She began putting away her notebook. When she looked up again, a small boy was standing in front of her. He seemed to have appeared from nowhere. Wayne and Murphy had heard the entire conversation. Wayne could almost taste the money he could make out of this.

"How much would it be worth to you if I followed the kid? I could find out where he goes; who he knows. I might even find this Kelly. You'll need some cor-ro-bor-a-ting evidence." He struggled over the long word. Kate laughed.

"You've been watching too much TV."

"TV, miss? No, but I've spent a lot of time in police stations."

Kate sobered up. He was right. The truth was that she couldn't print much of a story without some kind of confirmation of the facts. If she got her facts wrong the paper would be sued for a fortune. They just wouldn't risk it. "OK," she said, "here's my card. Find out what you can. We'll negotiate a price depending on what you get." Wayne was satisfied and turned to go. Then he stopped and turned back. "That man don't work for no gallery, miss. They all wear uniforms and they don't 'ave guns. If you've got any in-crim-in-a-ting evidence you'd better leg it!" he said and darted away.

Up till then it hadn't occurred to Kate that she might be in any danger. She told herself to walk calmly out of the room. She mustn't attract attention to herself. She forced herself to walk slowly over to where a uniformed security guard was standing. She dialled her own answer machine at work and played back the recording into her mobile. Then she rang one of her colleagues at the office.

"Tom, just listen. I need you to come and meet me at the gallery. If I'm not here when you get here go back to the office and print the story that's on my answer machine. You can use my disappearance as corroborating evidence."

"What on earth…" he began.

"Just shut up and get here fast, I think I may be in danger."

*

Worcestershire

Christine walked slowly back towards home. She had just dropped the boys off at school. She was in a thoughtful mood. It had been an exciting start to the day. They had all got up early to watch Emma open her presents. It had become a family tradition. Emma had gone off to school in a happy mood. Christine didn't really like the idea of having the party down in Worcester. But it seemed to be the 'in thing'. She had to accept it. She was looking forward to having a quiet meal out with Paul. The babysitter for Jake had already been booked.

The sun burst through the clouds. The rays lit up the church tower. It was like one of those moments from a movie. Christine laughed at the thought. As a family they walked the fifty yards to church on Christmas Eve, Christmas Day and Easter Day. Like most people Sundays were filled with transporting the children to swimming, or gymnastics or trampolining. The afternoons were for getting the weekend homework done.

Christine wondered if it was a sign, and felt a little foolish at the thought. She made a detour. She went through the gates of the churchyard. She heard her feet scrunching on the gravel path. Apart from her footsteps, the air was perfectly still. As she went into the porch she wondered if the door would be locked. She lifted the latch and it opened.

Inside the church it was cold. But it was also very peaceful.

Christine went near the front and sat on a pew. She let her eyes wander around. She saw things she hadn't noticed when the church was full of people. She read some of the inscriptions on the walls about people who had worshipped there years ago. The sun came out again. It streamed in through a side window. The altar and cross lit up. "Just like a Hollywood movie," Christine said to herself. Then she did something she hadn't done since she was a little girl. She prayed. It was only one prayer. It was simple. It was for Timothy.

*

London

Tim couldn't understand why they were being made to leave. The gallery didn't usually bother about vagrants if they were quiet and clean. He supposed it was because of all the special guests. His arm was hurting where the man was gripping it. Simon was objecting. "You have no right to do this," he said. "It's an open gallery." The man stopped and swung around, dragging Tim with him. He pulled back his jacket to reveal a revolver tucked into his belt. "This gives me the right," he growled. Simon said nothing. Tim was confused. Why did the security guard have a gun? It didn't make any sense to him. They were forced down a back stair. Tim was pushed through a door into a small storeroom. There were boxes everywhere and Tim was shoved into a pile of them. Simon was ordered to follow. Tim could see that Simon was worried.

Simon wasn't just worried. He was scared.

"What on earth is going on?" he asked. "Who do you work for?"

The man sneered at Simon, "Mr Edwards. Stupid tramp."

"Why does he need all this security?" asked Simon. "He's just a TV presenter."

The man sniggered. "You really don't know, do you? He's not just any presenter. He's **the** TV presenter. Every channel

68

on the planet wants to hire him. He earns more than all the other presenters put together. He's worth more than the Prime Minister. He's probably worth more than the Queen."

Simon began to realise the danger they were in. "How much is he paying you?" he asked.

"More than you can imagine," was the smug reply.

"What do you want with us?" Simon asked, although he thought he could guess.

"You saw something you shouldn't have. My orders are to dispose of the evidence. It'll look like an accident. No one will miss a couple of vagrants," he said matter-of-factly.

"You would protect a murderer just for money?" Simon couldn't really believe it. This kind of thing didn't happen in England.

"For what he's paying me, I'll do anything I'm told."

Now Simon understood. This was a life or death situation. He looked across at Tim's terrified face. He had to save the boy. It was his fault they were here. They should have gone straight back to Martin's house. His feelings of guilt welled up inside and became a terrible rage. Simon launched himself at the man, regardless of his own safety. The man was caught off guard and fell crashing to the floor. Simon grabbed the edges of the man's jacket and pulled them upwards, pinning his arms inside.

"Run Tim!" he shouted. "Go to Martin. Quick, his address is in my pocket. If he isn't there, go to Paddington station. Go back, Tim, and find your family." Simon paused to wrestle with the man, trying to keep him pinned down using all the weight of his large frame. "Hurry, I can't hold him for long."

Tim delved into Simon's pocket and found Martin's piece of paper. He put his arms around Simon's neck and hugged him. Tears were streaming down his face.

"Run, Tim, run!" Simon said in a strangled voice.

Tim fled.

Part Six

London

Tim ran. He wasn't exactly sure what he was running from. He still didn't really understand what was going on. But Simon had told him to run. So he ran. He ran till he could run no longer. He finally stopped for a rest near some shops. He would be safe with other people around. He didn't know if anyone had followed him. He went into a shoe shop and looked at some trainers. Then he sat on one of the chairs put out for customers. He took Martin's piece of paper out of his pocket. He could just about read the address. Tim remembered the roads near Martin's house, but he had no idea which direction it was.

He hadn't noticed which way he had been running. He might have been going in the opposite direction. He would have to ask someone.

They weren't much help in the shoe shop. But they could give directions to a post office. Tim ran to the post office.

At the post office, Tim had to queue. He felt safe among all the people. Now he had time to think. Simon had told him to go to Martin's. Martin would know what to do. He hoped Simon would be OK. Simon hadn't seen anything; he wasn't 'evidence'. Surely the man in shades could let him go. They could meet up at Martin's. Simon would be able to explain everything to Martin. The queue moved slowly. Tim had plenty of time to recover his breath. He looked out of the window. He caught a glimpse of a man in a suit and shades. He didn't look like the same man. But Tim was sure he had been followed. It was him they were after. They wouldn't do anything to him while he was in the post office.

Finally it was his turn at the counter. A young woman patiently got out a map and gave him directions. She kindly wrote them down for Tim.

Now what? Tim wouldn't be able to outrun the man. He looked at the directions. They were written in large loopy handwriting. It was easy to read. He checked which direction he had to go first. He looked around, trying to decide how to slip past the man. Then he noticed a side access for disabled people. He decided to wait in there; if he waited long enough, the man might think he had missed him. He might give up and leave. Tim went through the automatic doors and waited on the ramp. He could see from where he was if the man came in to look for him.

Tim made himself wait until a man on a mobility scooter used the exit. Then he crouched down and ran alongside. He was hoping that the man would turn in the direction Tim wanted to go. He didn't. Tim stood up and ran again. This time he ran with a purpose. He followed the directions carefully. Every now and again he would dive into a crowded shop and make himself rest. Then he would wait for a family with a buggy or a large person to leave and squeeze out with them.

Eventually the roads became familiar. Now Tim knew his way. Martin's house came into view. Tim ran up the steps with a feeling of relief. He rang the doorbell. He rang it again... and again. No one answered. Martin wasn't at home. Tim had just expected Martin to open the door straight away. He had half expected him to be waiting for him. He had thought he was safe now. He had thought he could rest now. He could feel a lump in his throat. He wanted to cry. His legs were so tired he could hardly stand. It wasn't fair. Why wasn't Martin home?

Tim couldn't run any more. He sat down on the doorstep. He could just wait till Martin got home. But he didn't know how long that would be. Simon had told him to go to Paddington station if Martin wasn't there. He had told him to go back and find his family. Simon must have meant that he should catch a train back to Birmingham. But he had no money to buy a ticket. What would he do if he got there? What if he didn't have a family? If he went to the police they would take him back to the home. Tim decided to wait for now. He felt horribly lonely. He missed Simon. If he waited here, Simon would know where to find him.

Tim sat on the doorstep long enough to get very cold. He kept looking up and down the road for Martin or Simon. They hadn't had much to eat today. He was hungry. He was worried about Simon. Surely, thought Tim, he should be here by now. He hoped Martin hadn't gone away. Simon had told Tim to go to Paddington if Martin wasn't home. Tim began to wonder why he hadn't told him to meet him somewhere. He wanted to stay with Simon. Then he began to wonder if Simon thought he was too much trouble. Maybe he should just go.

Tim's mind was made up for him. A large black saloon car pulled up. Two men got out. They were wearing suits and shades. Tim didn't hesitate. He ran down the steps. He dodged away as one of them reached for him and ran.

Tim had no idea how to get to Paddington. He just kept running, and chose roads that had dead ends where cars couldn't go. He ran through alleyways and one-way streets. He crossed dual carriageways. He ran till he recognised a street. Now he knew where he was. These roads were on Simon's routes. He made his way to Oxford Street where he knew he could get lost in the crowds. He knew where there were side roads that he could cut through. The only way anyone could have followed would have been on foot.

Tim decided to find his way to Hyde Park. There were plenty of places to hide. He knew his way around. He knew where he could shelter for the night if he needed to. He still had his rucksack with his bed stuffed inside. Simon would look for him there if he didn't find him at Martin's. He knew the way. Tim ran.

*

Wayne was excited. He ran up to Murphy. "Quick, follow me an' stay out of sight." Murphy was used to obeying Wayne's orders without question. He ran close behind. His soft trainers made no noise. There was nothing Wayne enjoyed more than a good chase. It was usually him being chased. This time he wasn't in any danger. This time he might make a lot of money. Wayne watched as Tim was pushed into the storeroom. He and Murphy waited out of sight. They heard the commotion and watched as Tim ran from the room. They followed him out of the building. Outside, Wayne suddenly grabbed Murphy and pulled him back. "'Ang on," he said, "someone else is followin' 'im, look." Wayne pointed to another man in suit and shades. The man was clearly following Tim.

"This'll make it easier for us," said Wayne, "we just follow the suit."

Murphy just nodded as usual. He didn't look very enthusiastic. Wayne laughed at him. "C'mon, I reckon this'll be a good little earner." They set off in pursuit. They followed Tim and the 'suit' to the shoe shop. Then they followed them to the post office. Tim seemed to be in there a very long time.

"'E must've lost 'im," said Murphy gloomily.

"Nah, it's just a long queue. 'Aven't you ever been in a post office?" Wayne asked, showing off his superior knowledge.

They could see the suit waiting outside. He kept making calls on his mobile. He was pacing up and down impatiently. They watched as Tim nearly gave him the slip as he came out. "Good plan," observed Wayne, "shame the old guy went the wrong way." Tim was moving faster now. Wayne was worried that the suit would lose him. If that happened they would be too far away to see him themselves.

"I think 'e knows where 'e's goin' now. We'd better nobble the suit quick or we might lose 'im," said Wayne between breaths as they ran. "I'll run past 'im so I can get my eyes on Tim. You nobble the suit and keep 'im down as long as you can, OK? We'll meet back at our bench, right?"

"OK," said Murphy, "but I'm gettin' 'ungry, so don't be long."

Wayne laughed. "You're always 'ungry. You just stop the suit catchin' up an' I'll see you later." Wayne summoned the energy to sprint off.

Murphy tried to keep up. He watched Wayne run past the suit. Murphy had to think of a plan, quick. The man was at least six foot tall and broad shouldered. Murphy wouldn't be able to just trip him up. He had to think, quickly. He wasn't used to it. Wayne did all the thinking. Murphy knew he was good at diversions... He smiled to himself as he thought of a plan. Wayne would be proud of him.

Murphy got closer. When he was about two metres away he slowed down. Then he waited for the right moment. There was a lady coming towards him with a large shoulder bag. Wayne had taught him how to grab a bag from the shoulder. With one swift move Murphy had the bag. He made no effort to conceal it. The lady could see exactly who had taken it. Then Murphy ran at the suit. He threw himself at him hard enough to make him stumble. As he did so, he shoved the bag into the man's hands. He shouted, "'Ere you are, gov'!" then darted into an alleyway and disappeared.

The owner of the bag and half a dozen witnesses ran up to the man in shades. The lady demanded the return of her bag. Someone was shouting for the police. Several bystanders helped to restrain the man while a helpful shop assistant rang the police. The suit was going nowhere.

Wayne kept close to Tim. Every now and again, Tim stopped to look at a piece of paper. He was obviously following directions. This made it easy for Wayne. He watched Tim run up the steps at Martin's house. He made a mental note of the address. It would be something to sell to the reporter later.

Wayne had learnt patience over the years. But he nearly gave up. Tim must be waiting for someone. Wayne wanted to see who it was. He was just wondering about crossing the road to keep Tim company, when the black car pulled up. Wayne saw the suits getting out. He saw Tim make his getaway. Then he set off once more in pursuit.

*

Martin ran up the steps to his front door. He looked at his watch. He had expected to be home hours ago. The meeting had seemed to go on forever. He was tired and grumpy. It had been an important meeting. He was glad he had been invited. But now he needed a strong cup of tea. He let himself in and looked at the answer machine. There was one message. He pressed the playback button. Someone had started to speak but had changed their mind and hung up. Martin hoped it wasn't Simon. If he'd tried to ring while he was out he might not try again.

Martin couldn't get Tim out of his head. It was so wrong that some children were forced to live on the streets. The meeting that afternoon had been about runaways in London. He had made some suggestions. He hoped something would come of it. He made a pot of tea, poured himself a cup, and then reached up for the biscuit tin. As he did so the phone rang. He wondered if it would be Simon this time.

"Hello, can I help you?" he asked.

"I hope so," came the reply, "my name is Paul Whittaker, and I think my son was staying with you."

Paul had a lot of questions. He knew Chris would ask all these and probably more later. Martin told him everything he knew. He told Paul about Tim's made-up story about a family with two houses and a brother called Carl. "I don't think he remembers much of his real family. The only thing he was sure about was his old bear. I don't know why he ran away from the children's home. There was a lot he didn't tell me. I wouldn't have let him leave with the old man if I hadn't trusted him. I could tell that he genuinely cares for Tim. He has been looking after him for a couple of months now."

Paul wanted Martin to describe exactly what Tim looked like. What was his hair like? How tall was he? Did he look healthy? What was he wearing? Martin did his best to answer all these questions. He wished he had taken a photograph. "One thing I can tell you," he said, "he likes sausages for breakfast." They both laughed. "Look, as I told Mrs Griffiths, they have my address and phone number. They know they can come here if they need help. I regularly visit the places where they can get handouts. I'll pass the word around to look out for them. If you let me have a contact number, I'll ring you if I hear anything at all."

Paul gave Martin his home, office and mobile numbers.

"You can call me any time, day or night," he said, "and thanks."

Martin put the phone down. He looked out of the window. It was already beginning to get dark. "How do people survive out there in the cold?" he wondered. "How will they find Tim now?" Martin knelt down and prayed.

*

Kelly woke up. She felt rough. Business had been good last night. She had crashed out after her fix in the morning and then slept for the rest of the day. It was only four o'clock. She had plenty of time to get ready for another shift. It was Friday. There were always a lot of clients on Fridays. The other girls at Paddington had bitched about the way she looked. Her face was still swollen. It would take time to get ready. Dave wouldn't be back until six. She had the flat to herself for a while. It would be a good chance to go through her clothes. Apart from a pair of old pyjamas, all her clothes were for work. She took everything out of the drawers and laid them out on the settee. Clearly she needed some new clothes. She picked out the best ones and put them to one side. She would wear those tonight. Then she checked to see how much cash she had left from last night. There was enough for a cheap meal and a new outfit. She threw a few clothes away to make room in the drawer. If she got dressed straight away, she'd have time to go shopping before work.

Kelly had learnt the hard way that she had to pay for her clothes. It wasn't worth the risk to pinch them. She couldn't afford to spend any time at the police station when she could be working. Anyway, spending money on good working clothes was an investment. It would pay for itself. She would be more likely to attract wealthier clients.

It had been a while since she had been shopping. She was looking forward to it. It was a chance to do something normal. It was a chance to do something for herself. She found herself humming a happy tune, as she got dressed. She also needed to buy some more foundation. Since having her face bashed in she needed to use a lot more to cover up the scars. She was still humming when she went into the bathroom to do her makeup. Even the stink in that room didn't spoil her feeling of excitement.

When she stepped out onto the street there was a smile on her face. It didn't happen very often. Kelly headed for Oxford Street. She told herself not to go any further than Regent Street. It wouldn't seem so far to go back to Paddington. She wouldn't have time to go as far as Tottenham Court Road this afternoon. She didn't want to rush.

A short while later, Kelly strolled into a boutique. She was looking for a top that might keep her a bit warmer. It still needed to be enticing. She found a long red fluffy tunic top. It was long enough to wear as a short dress but she could also wear it with trousers. She took it to the 'pay here' desk. She didn't see Tim run by. But she did notice the TV up in the corner. The sound was turned down very low, but the picture was clear enough. A ridiculous pink satin suit caught her eye. She found herself looking at the screen. It was some sort of celebrity. He was cutting a ribbon. It looked like some kind of opening ceremony. Kelly thought he looked stupid. She turned to the shop assistant.

"Who on earth is that?" she asked disdainfully.

The shop assistant looked up at the screen. "Don't you know?" she said in surprise.

"Why do people always say that?" thought Kelly to herself, "If I knew who he was, I wouldn't have asked."

Out loud, she said, "No, I've never seen him before."

"It's Ross Edwards, the TV presenter," said the shop assistant knowingly, "he's over at the Tate opening a new exhibition."

The camera zoomed in on his face. Kelly saw that she had been wrong. She had seen him before. He wasn't wearing pink last time. He didn't have that stupid smile on his face last time. Neither did he have that silly hair. But it was the same face. She would never forget that. Kelly imagined herself running into the Tate. She would yell at the top of her voice. She would tell all those reporters what he was really like. Everyone would hate him as much as she did. But she knew no one would believe her in real life. She would probably be locked up herself for something. She turned away and tried to put him out of her mind. A few minutes later, Kelly was heading back up Oxford Street. She would think about where to eat, instead.

*

Worcestershire

It was already dark outside. Emma still hadn't decided what to wear. She had already tried on a dozen outfits. Her shoes were all out on the floor in a row. She needed help. Emma reached for her mobile and sent a text to Sarah. Then she went downstairs to wait for her friend.

Christine was in the kitchen preparing an early tea for Jake. Emma went in and put the kettle on.

"Cup of tea, Mum?" she asked.

"Yes please, and how about a toasted teacake to keep us going?" suggested Christine.

Emma sliced the teacakes and put them in the toaster while she made a pot of tea. She got out her mum's favourite teacup and a mug for herself. She toasted a teacake for Jake as well. She sat down at the long farmhouse table. She watched the butter melting on the teacake. Christine came and sat down with her. "So much for the diet," she sighed, "never mind, it's a special day. Is everyone coming tonight?"

Emma had told her mum about Luke. She didn't like to keep secrets from her. She always seemed to find out anyway.

"Yes, everyone's coming. I've asked Sarah to come over early to help me get dressed. I can't decide what to wear."

Christine laughed. "You mean you've got too many clothes to choose from!"

Emma changed the subject. "What are you and Dad doing tonight?" she asked.

"Your Dad is taking me out for a nice quiet meal at the Masons Arms. Hopefully Jake will be fast asleep by the time we get back. We should have a nice quiet evening." Christine smiled at Emma as she picked up her dripping teacake. Then she asked, "Who's driving tonight?"

Emma couldn't stop herself blushing. "Luke is coming here to pick up Sarah and me. He said he could bring us back too."

"Well at least he knows the way," was Christine's only response.

Emma pictured Luke in her mind. He had told her that he had only had one girlfriend before, while he was still at school. Emma liked that thought. She secretly wanted the fairy-tale wedding. She wanted to keep herself for 'The One'. The doorbell rang. Emma went to let Sarah in. She ran back into the kitchen and gulped down the last of her tea. Then she took Sarah upstairs with her.

"The thing is," explained Emma, "I don't want to get cold. I look really pale and sickly if I get too cold. That's the trouble with having a birthday in winter. It's all right for you. You can have a barbeque or a swimming party. It's just not the same in winter."

Sarah was helpful. They decided on an outfit with enough layers to keep warm. She would be able to peel them off later and show off her new top. Next they chose the shoes. Sarah offered to curl Emma's hair for her. The only thing left was the makeup.

Now that the difficult decisions had been made, Emma relaxed. She took her time over her makeup. Sarah had brought her makeup bag with her. They sat in front of the mirror to-gether. They debated the best kind of mascara and pondered over the right shade of eye shadow.

Once satisfied with how they looked, Emma checked her watch. It was still an hour till Luke was due to pick them up. She could feel the excitement bubbling up. Emma sent a few last-minute texts to her friends. She didn't want anyone saying they had forgotten. Then they went downstairs and sat down in front of the TV to wait. Christine had left the news channel on.

"Look," said Sarah, "It's Ross Edwards. No one else would dare wear a pink satin suit in public."

"Ugh," said Emma in a voice of distaste, "I don't know why everyone makes such a fuss about him. He's not even good looking."

"He's very funny," said Sarah. "Did you see him presenting the music awards last week? He did a brilliant take-off of that new band from Scunthorpe. I was in stitches."

"I just think he's stupid," said Emma as she picked up the remote and changed channels. Emma liked men to be like… Luke.

*

London

It was already dark by the time Tim reached Hyde Park. He decided to go straight to one of Simon's favourite benches. He knew the way. He hoped Simon would look for him there. He couldn't run any more. He had to rest. He saw the bench, but there was someone already there. It was a small person. It wasn't Simon. Tim walked despondently over to the bench. He sat down at one end. He didn't look at the other person. He just drew his legs up and curled into a ball.

As Tim cooled down after all his running; he began to shiver. He wondered if he should wait for Simon. Should he just do what Simon had told him and go to Paddington? He didn't know the way. He would wait, for now. But he knew he couldn't wait for long. It was too cold.

Less than a minute later Wayne strolled into view. Murphy watched him approach. He jumped up and ran to meet him.

"'E just turned up on our bench!" Murphy said excitedly.

"If I'd known where 'e was g'nna go I could've saved meself a lot o' trouble," was Wayne's disgruntled reply.

Tim had watched them. As they got closer, he recognised them. Maybe they could tell him the way to Paddington. Tim was surprised when they walked straight up to him. He'd only met them once before and only for a moment. He hadn't expected them to remember him.

"You're Tim, yeah?" Wayne said. It was more of a statement than a question.

"Ye-es," replied Tim, trying to remember the boy's name.

"I'm Wayne, remember?"

"Yes," said Tim again.

"Right, well we've gotta talk. We need a plan to get you safe somewhere. Those suits that are after you, they might 'ave lost you for now, but they 'eard the old man tell you to go to Paddington, same as I did. They'll be waitin' for you."

Tim was confused. What did Wayne have to do with all this?

"Have you seen Simon? Where is he?" he asked.

"Is that the old man? I dunno where 'e is or what's 'appened to 'im. But you could be worth a lot o' money to me, so I gotta keep you safe, yeah?"

Tim really had no idea what Wayne was talking about. He knew he should go to Paddington station; he would have to risk it. Wayne seemed to want to help. "I've got to go to Paddington station. I've gotta catch a train to Birmingham," Tim said with more determination than he felt. Wayne shrugged his shoulders. If the kid was going to insist, he'd just have to figure out a way to out-manoeuvre the suits.

"OK," he said, "we'll take you there. We can 'ang around with the working girls for a while. They won't be lookin' for you there. Then we'll work out a plan. You'll be safe with us. Me and Murphy, we're the best."

Murphy grinned at Tim. Tim got up off the bench to go with them.

"What about food?" asked Murphy, "I'm 'ungry."

"I'm starvin'," agreed Tim.

"I'm buyin'," said Wayne.

*

Simon had held the man down as long as he could. A second man came into the room and pulled him off. He punched Simon in the stomach. Simon was winded and crumpled to the floor. They began making phone calls, describing Tim. Then they turned back to Simon. He knew what was coming next.

"Right, where's the boy gone?"

Simon knew he had to give Tim time to get to Martin's house. He hoped he would hold out long enough. He knew he would tell them in the end. People always do. He just needed to give Tim enough time to get there. The pain began.

Lifting his head, Simon could see it was getting dark outside the window. Tim must have got there by now. He could tell them Martin's address now. Martin would know what to do. He could stop the pain now.

The pain stopped. The men left the room. They left Simon where he lay. They turned off the light and locked him in. Why didn't they let him go now? They had what they wanted. Simon lay in a heap on the floor. In the darkness he drifted in and out of consciousness. In his semi-conscious state he began to see faces. He saw his wife smiling at him. It was how she had looked when he had first seen her. He saw the faces of his two children. They had stayed the same age in his memory. He saw the boy he had knocked down. Then other faces drifted by. People he had met down the years. Then came Tim. He saw Tim standing there in the gents at Victoria. He saw him eating breakfast at Maggie's. He saw him laughing with Kelly. Then he

83

saw him frightened.

As he lay there in the dark, Simon looked back over his life. What had he done with it? What had he achieved? He had just been surviving. Until he had met Tim, his life had been meaningless. It had had no purpose. Tim had become his friend. He had become like a son. The door opened. Simon's swollen eyes were blinded by the sudden light.

"OK, old man. We heard you tell the boy to go to Paddington. Where's he going? Where's he catching a train to?"

"I don't know," said Simon. It was half true. He presumed it would be back to Birmingham, but he didn't know for sure. Tim hadn't told him much. It could have been anywhere. Simon realised that they must have got to Martin's too late. Tim had got away. He supposed Martin wasn't home, but Tim had followed his advice to go back. Now he realised that he had achieved something. He had helped Tim to survive all these weeks. He had taught him about things he didn't know. He had shown him things that most people never saw. And he had helped him to escape from these evil people. He smiled to himself.

The pain began again. Simon knew he wouldn't speak this time. He knew this time he would win. As he lost consciousness, an old saying he remembered from his childhood went through his head: 'greater love has no man than this, than that he lay down his life for his friend.' Tim was his friend.

The park attendant who was to find Simon's body the next morning wouldn't be surprised. This time of year he often found vagrants that had frozen to death overnight. It was part of his job to clear up. No one ever missed them. No one ever wondered. No one ever asked any questions.

Part Seven

London

Wayne led Tim and Murphy on a circuitous route to Paddington station. "Just in case," he said. He didn't think they had been followed, but they kept to the shadows. Wayne took them to where the girls congregated, waiting for their Friday night clients. He left them there while he went to get something to eat. "Just keep out o' sight," he recommended.

Tim and Murphy stood back in the shadows and waited. Neither of them spoke. Tim was frightened and Murphy was tired. A short while later, Wayne came back with some packets of crisps, sausage rolls and a couple of cans of coke. Tim didn't ask any questions. He'd learnt that from Simon. He was just glad to have something to eat. They squatted down with their backs to a wall.

"I didn't see any suits," said Wayne. "D'you know where you're goin', Tim?"

"I've got to catch a train to Birmingham," said Tim. "But I don't have any money to buy a ticket," he added gloomily.

"Don't worry," said Wayne optimistically, "we'll get you on that train. While we're thinkin' about that, you can tell me all about the celebrity in the pink suit." Wayne wanted all the details. The more he knew, the more information he would have to sell. By the time Tim had finished telling him about what he'd seen, Wayne wanted more than just money. He wanted this Ross Edwards to suffer in public. These girls were the closest thing to a family for Wayne. They lived in his world. They played the same games. One of the girls walked over to them.

"Hello Tim, remember me?" she asked.

Tim looked up. It was Kelly. Tim introduced them all. Wayne remembered that Kate had been asking about Kelly. He made a mental note of her name and face. He would want to talk to her later. He was sure they could both profit from this.

"Tim's in trouble," Wayne explained. "There are some guys in suits who are after 'im 'cause 'e's a witness to a crime. 'E needs to get a train to Birmingham before it's too late!" he said dramatically.

Kelly laughed. She doubted that it was as serious as Wayne said. "I'll help you get on the train Tim, if someone is really after you," she said in an amused voice. "They won't recognise me and they'll be expecting you to be on your own. We'll need to get you a change of clothes and a different hat. But you'll be on your own once you're on the train. I'll go and get a ticket," she said.

Murphy was made to swap jackets with Tim and Wayne reluctantly swapped hats.

"I'll get on the train with Tim and then I'll get off again just before it leaves. You two watch out for the bad guys," Kelly said in a mock conspiratorial voice.

"Yeah, we can nobble them!" said Murphy enthusiastically.

Kelly took Tim's hand. "C'mon, we'll look like brother and sister."

The train was crowded with commuters. They went to the furthest carriage, but there were still no seats. "They probably won't bother checking tickets with all these people in the way," Kelly said, "and it'll make it easier for you to keep out of sight if these guys have followed you on to the train." They found a place to stand, and waited.

Wayne and Murphy watched while Kelly led Tim into the station. There were hundreds of people hurrying towards the trains. Wayne realised they wouldn't be able to see the suits in the crowd. They would just have to hope the suits would have just as much trouble spotting Tim. It was a long time before they saw Kelly coming back. She looked fed up. "It's OK, he's safe on the train and the train has gone now. It was delayed. We had to wait ages. I'm glad I don't have to do that every day!" Wayne looked relieved. "OK," said Kelly, "now you can tell me what's going on. Where's the old man? What did Tim see, and what's in it for you?"

*

Tim slid to the floor as the train pulled out of the station. He couldn't stand any longer. He shuffled into a corner and hoped no one would tread on him. Even if the men had followed him, they couldn't do much on this crowded train. He was safe for now. It was warm on the train. Tim began to relax. He hoped it would be a long journey. He was in no hurry to get off. He realised he would probably never see Kelly again, or Wayne, or Murphy. Maybe one day he might visit Martin again; he knew his address. He didn't think he would ever forget it. What about Simon? He knew all the places Simon would go. He was sure he would remember the places he stopped for his freebies. He missed Simon.

A familiar feeling of loneliness began to creep over Tim. It hadn't been there the whole time he was with Simon. Now he was on his own again. He wouldn't go back to the children's home. Maybe he could find another friend like Simon in Birmingham. Although he'd lived all his life in Birmingham, he didn't know it the way he knew London now. He wouldn't know where it was safe to sleep. He wouldn't know where to get any freebies. He didn't know the names of any of the roads in the city centre. He didn't know where the galleries were. Who would sit and look at paintings with him if he found them? He didn't know where the parks were. He didn't know anything. Perhaps he wouldn't get off at Birmingham. He would just stay on the train and see where it went.

Tim didn't recognise the names of any of the places where

they stopped until they reached Oxford. He had heard of that. A lot of people got off at Oxford. Tim finally found a seat and curled up in the corner. He took Bear out of his rucksack and looked at him. "Well, old Bear, it's just you and me again," he said. He shut his eyes and drifted into a fitful sleep.

*

Worcestershire

The babysitter had arrived on time. Christine went to get her coat. It was a cold night, so she picked up a scarf and her driving gloves. Christine had offered to drive back, so that Paul could have a drink. She glanced in the mirror and smoothed down some flyaway hair. She gave some last-minute instructions to Jake and picked up her handbag. Paul was already at the door, waiting. He seemed unusually excited. It wasn't an anniversary, other than Emma's birthday. There would be no reason for any surprises. Christine couldn't guess what he might be up to. She wasn't going to spoil it for him by asking. She just got into the car without a word.

It was only a five-minute journey to the Masons Arms and neither of them spoke a word. It was unusual for them. Paul went ahead of Christine and held the door open for her. She could sense his excitement as she went past. The waitress ushered them to their table and brought their usual drinks.

"Shall we order first?" asked Paul.

"Before what?" asked Christine, no longer able to contain her curiosity.

"I have something to tell you," he said evasively.

"Good or bad?" asked Christine.

"You'll have to judge that for yourself," replied Paul.

Christine was baffled. "Yes, let's order first. Will I still feel like eating, though?"

"Don't worry. It isn't that bad," Paul assured her.

They studied the menu. It was a waste of time; neither of them could think about food. In the end they chose the same thing they had last time they were there.

"It's about Timothy," said Paul, "he's alive!"

Christine went a funny colour. "There's going to be a 'but'," she said.

Paul told Christine the whole story, as he knew it up to that time. He told her about his conversation with Bob and about his meeting with Mrs Griffiths. He recounted the phone call with Mrs Griffiths and then with Martin. He remembered all the details. He was able to answer all her questions. "And he still has Bear," he finished. The waitress brought their meals.

They both sat in silence for a while just staring at the food.

"So we have to just wait for this old man to bring Timothy back to the minister? Isn't there anything we can do?" asked Christine.

"I only spoke to Reverend Allen this afternoon. I haven't had a chance to do anything else yet. I wanted to tell you first. I thought we could start by ringing the local police stations. Reverend Allen is going to visit all the hostels tomorrow and I think we should go down to London as soon as we can arrange it. We'll find him, I promise you."

Christine sank her head into her hands and sobbed. After a few minutes she went to the ladies and washed her face. She came back to the table and picked up her knife and fork. "Right," she said with renewed energy, "we'd better eat this. We'll need all our strength. We've got a huge task ahead of us." She smiled at Paul, a smile that he hadn't seen for a long time.

*

Worcester

The movie had finished. Emma and her friends drifted out, chatting happily. They were comparing it to the last Bond movie. Some of them preferred the old style Bond. Some of them had fallen for the new. They were all happy and hungry as they strolled towards the Pizza Place. Luke and Emma walked hand in hand. They had discovered they had a lot in common. They both liked reading. They liked the same kind of music and they both enjoyed going to the theatre.

They ordered their food and sat in a group. Emma was horribly embarrassed when they all sang Happy Birthday to her. One by one her friends came over and gave her presents. There was a lot of jewellery. Luke gave her a bracelet. Emma was enjoying herself hugely.

"Heard anything about your brother yet?" asked her friend Rachel. A shadow passed over Emma's face. "No, but thanks for asking." Emma would rather people didn't ask about Timothy. It stirred up too many unhappy thoughts.

"I can see it's not something you want to talk about," said Luke, "but if you tell me the whole story now, we won't have to talk about it again and I'll know all about you." He looked genuinely interested. If they were going to be friends, he'd need to know. She'd have to tell him, if only to protect her Mum and Dad. After all, it wasn't a secret. It had been all over the TV. Emma sighed.

"Timothy was three when he went missing," she began. "I used to help Mum look after him, especially when Jake was born. I remember what he looked like then. But I don't suppose I would recognise him now. He had a favourite teddy bear called Bear. He wouldn't give it a proper name. All my bears have names like Humphrey or Fudge or... don't laugh! Anyway, Timothy insisted his name was Bear. He had it with him when he went missing. Bear was never found either. The police did their best to find him but..." Emma was interrupted as Luke's mobile rang. He looked to see who was calling. "Sorry," he apologised, "I'll have to take this call. I'll go outside where it's a bit quieter."

Emma watched him get up and go. Every year when it was Timothy's birthday, the family would gather in his bedroom. They would each put a present on his bed, "just in case," said Mum. It got harder each year trying to think what he might like. Trying to imagine what sort of boy he had become. They were all sure he was alive somewhere.

Luke came back. "I'm really sorry, Em, one of my customers has a burst pipe. Is there any chance your Mum can come down and collect you? Don't worry, I'll stay with you till she gets here. But these people live on the other side of Worcester. If I take you home first it'll be more than an hour before I get there."

Emma liked the way Luke already called her 'Em', as if he'd known her for years. "I'm sure it'll be fine," she said, and picked up her mobile. She sent a text. Luke looked anxious. "It's OK, don't worry. Go and be a hero," said Emma. A text came back. "She said she'll come as soon as they've paid the bill. You needn't wait."

Luke insisted on waiting while they quickly finished eating and paid. Then he walked with Emma and Sarah to the Odeon. There was a lay-by outside, where Christine could pull in to pick them up. They sat down on the steps opposite the station to wait.

*

London

Kate was at her laptop, working late in her office. She had typed up the all-too-short interview with Tim. Now she was trying to find out as much background as she could on Ross Edwards. If what the kid had told her was true, then she would find something. She just had to keep digging. Tom had agreed to stay around till she went home. He could see that she was scared. The details of the kid's story rang too true for fiction. Tom was doing some research into the lives of homeless kids for some extra background.

The phone rang. Kate finished typing her sentence, then picked up.

"Hello?"

"Is that Kate?"

"Yes."

"My name is Wayne. We met at the gallery this afternoon."

Kate put the phone onto speaker so that Tom could listen in. She also set it to record.

"What do you have for me, Wayne?" asked Kate.

"I've got the address of a house that Tim went to. I dunno who lives there; there was no one in. The suits followed 'im there and tried to grab 'im again. He got away. I helped 'im get to a station."

"Which one?" interrupted Kate.

"You'll get all those details when we've agreed a price," said Wayne, "I've got more."

"Go on," said Kate.

"I found Kelly. She's the girl Tim helped when this Ross Edwards bashed 'er face in. She said she'll talk to you if the price is right. And I can tell you where Tim was headed. By the way, Tim was on 'is own. They must've already done in the old man."

Kate thought for a moment. The boy could be in danger himself if he'd been seen. The only way they would all be safe would be if they could get the story out tonight. Any delay and Edwards could get a denial out first. He was popular enough to get away with it. "Listen, Wayne, we need to get this story in print tonight. It's the only way to protect all of us. Once it's in print he won't bother trying to harm us, because it would just prove our case. Can you bring Kelly over right now? Take a taxi. I'll pay for it when you get here. And don't worry, I'll make it worth your while. You can tell Kelly she'll get more for this than if she worked non-stop for a week. You've got the address on my card."

Wayne agreed and Kate hung up. She went to warn security that she was expecting guests. Then she went in to see the Editor. If he approved the story, this scoop would be the making of her. It would also rid the streets of at least one scumbag.

*

Worcestershire

Tim was woken up by the ticket inspector. "Tickets please," he demanded. "My Mum's got the tickets," lied Tim, "she's gone to the loo."

"I'll come back," said the inspector and moved on.

"Now what?" wondered Tim. He looked out of the window. It was pitch black. He couldn't see anything. He didn't have a clue where he was. The train seemed to be slowing. He could get off at the next station. He stuffed Bear into the top of his rucksack. Then he began walking down the train away from the inspector.

The train was definitely slowing. The driver announced the arrival at a station. Tim went and stood by the door. He could see the inspector coming back. The train still hadn't stopped. The inspector was getting closer. Tim didn't want to get caught now. The door opened. Tim stepped onto the platform with relief. The inspector didn't follow him off the train. The doors shut and the train pulled away.

Tim looked around. There was a sign saying 'Shrub Hill'. He'd never heard of it. He wondered if he'd gone as far as Scotland. There was already a train at another platform. Tim wondered where it was going. Then he noticed that someone else had got off the train. He was wearing a suit. He was watching Tim. Had he been followed all this way? Tim ran. He got to the other platform and jumped on the train. He went through the carriages to find one with a lot of people. What was he going to do? The man could have easily followed him on to this train. He couldn't keep running. He couldn't just stay on the train.

Tim decided to get off the train at the next stop. The man wouldn't be expecting that. He would sit as close as possible to the door. He would pretend to be asleep and at the last second, he would jump off. If he was quick enough, the man wouldn't be able to follow him. Tim sat down, closed his eyes and waited.

*

London

Kate picked up the phone and dialled the number. She was looking forward to this.

"Hello, can you put me through to Ross Edwards' publicist, please?" she asked.

"I'm sorry, she's not available at the moment. You'll have to try again in the morning," came the reply.

"What about his secretary or PA?" persisted Kate.

"I'm sorry, there's no one here." The voice was bored.

"Well, who are you?" asked Kate.

"I'm just a receptionist. If it's an emergency, I can give you a mobile number," she offered.

"Well it is," snapped Kate. Then she relented. It wasn't the receptionist's fault. "Yes please," she said, trying to sound friendly, "that would be very helpful."

Kate dialled again. This time she got straight through to the publicist.

"Hello?"

"Hello, my name is Kate Shipley from the 'Daily Journal'. I have a message for Ross Edwards. We're running a story in the morning. It has already gone to print. It is regarding his dealings with certain working girls. We have statements from eyewitnesses. He cannot stop the story now. The witnesses are under police protection. And one more thing; he might as well call off the hunt for the boy. I've already got his testimony." Kate hung up without waiting for a reply. This was the kind of journalism she enjoyed.

*

Worcestershire

Christine had been a little annoyed when she got Emma's text. She didn't blame Luke, but she had wanted time to think about what Paul had told her. She was looking forward to going home and spending the rest of the evening planning what to do next. Of course they had to go to London. She'd like to go tomorrow. She sent her reply to Emma and waited while Paul paid the bill. Paul didn't want to go with her. He asked Christine to drop him home first. He thought the girls would prefer to chat without Dad being there. Besides, he wanted to make some phone calls about Timothy.

Once again they made the short journey without speaking. Both were preoccupied with their own thoughts. Christine pulled onto the drive and waited until Paul had let himself in. It was just her luck that it was her turn to drive tonight. She would far rather have been at home.

Christine drove carefully. The road had a lot of sharp bends. She was tired. She knew she needed to be more careful. Once she reached the edge of Worcester, she was able to relax a bit. The streets were lit, so it was easier to see.

As she drove down past the University, she could see the Cathedral. It was lit up and there was a reflection in the river. She hoped Timothy wasn't near any rivers. She didn't know if he could swim. Christine drove over the bridge past the cricket ground. She wondered if Timothy played cricket. Paul loved the game. When Timothy was born, Paul had talked all the time about teaching him to play. She stopped at the lights. A few people were crossing the road. They were all wrapped up in big coats, scarves and gloves. She wondered if Timothy had warm clothes. She drove past the bus station and up towards the burger place. She wondered if Timothy was hungry. Then she turned the corner into Foregate Street. She hoped Emma would be waiting and ready to jump in. There was hardly ever any space in the lay-by outside the Odeon.

*

Worcester

Tim felt the train slowing down. He kept his eyes shut. He felt the train shudder to a stop. He heard the doors opening. He waited. Doors started to shut. He jumped up and ran for the door. He leapt onto the platform. He didn't stop to look to see if anyone had followed him.

Some other people had got off the train before Tim. He followed them to the exit. They went downstairs. He ran down behind them. He found himself standing on a pavement by a busy road. He was under a bridge. The railway crossed the road above him. He looked back over his shoulder. He couldn't see the man. Was he safe? He noticed a group of teenage boys.

They were making a lot of noise. As Tim stood, wondering what he should do next, one of the boys came up to him.

"Hey, what's this?" he asked, as he pulled Bear out of the top of Tim's rucksack. Tim felt a surge of panic. "Give him back," he yelled. The boy laughed and threw it to one of his friends. They began throwing it to each other, laughing at Tim's frantic efforts to get him back.

Then Tim heard a loud voice shouting from the other side of the road. "Hey, give the kid his bear." It was Luke.

The boy with Bear laughed unpleasantly. Then he threw Bear as hard as he could in the direction of the road. Bear hurtled through the air, his stuffed limbs flailing. His heavy beaded eyes weighed his head down so that he was flying head first towards a large muddy puddle. Tim knew that Bear was his. It was the only thing in his life that was really truly his. Tim could feel his heart racing. He could hardly breathe. He saw the car coming towards Bear and all he could see was his Bear in danger. He tried to run towards him but his legs felt like lead. Each step seemed to take forever. He was reaching for him now... he would catch him in time. There was a moment of intense relief as his fingers closed around the squashy toy, followed immediately by intense pain as his legs seemed to be cut from underneath him.

It was Tim's turn to hurtle through the air as the car screeched and skidded to a halt. Tim couldn't stand the pain and mercifully slipped into unconsciousness. The woman driver had leapt out of the car and rushed to see what had happened. She was now kneeling on the road cradling Tim's head in her lap and wailing hysterically: "It's Bear... it's Bear."

*

*

*

Timothy knew his name was Timothy Nathaniel Whittaker. He had always known it, but he hadn't thought about it for a long time. He seemed to be dreaming about his name. He could hear a woman saying his name over and over again. He decided to wake himself up because it was a silly dream. But he still seemed to be asleep, even though he thought he had opened his eyes.

"I know my name is Timothy Nathaniel Whittaker," he said. "Who are you?"

"Mummy," she replied.